For my precious garbling baby

ISBN: 1453860347
ISBN-13: 9781453860342

Preface

Okay, so this book is not really just all about my mother in-law. However, a small chunk of it is unconditionally devoted to a cold, devious feeling of animosity towards her. This is a story of a fifty-some-odd-year-old mother in-law who takes ultimate control of her near thirty-year-old daughter and baby granddaughter at the unrelenting expense of a her son in-law, who is forced to take extreme measures to ensure his place as a father to his beautiful, brand-new baby.

I would like to introduce myself. If you read the front cover, I'm sure you know my name, and I really hate repeating myself, so just flip it back over if you really don't remember. I'm a twenty-six-year-old man presently going through a divorce. My soon-to-be ex-wife and I have one daughter, who is only seven months old. I live in a four-bedroom, two-bath home in the Midwest with my beloved cat Doug. I am a full-time college student, and just because I have a federal tax identification number connected to an S-Corporation, which consequently I really don't do much with, I call myself a business owner.

That's the gist of it. Let me explain why we're here today. Life is a bitch, and then you marry her mother or find out you did, shortly after marrying her daughter. Holy crap, there truly is something to be said for in-laws.

"It Helps Fertility"

I stepped out of the house to grab a drink with a buddy at the bar, right down the street. It was about 8:00 pm. Later, at the bar, my phone rang, and I decided to step into the restroom of this dingy pub to answer it in a quiet place. My wife said, "Andrew! You need to come home. My water broke." All right then! We were three weeks early, damn near almost four weeks early.

"Honey, did you just pee yourself?" She insisted her water broke. I asked where and, of course...right in the toilet. So, as any man would, I promptly left the bar and sped home like a frantic turd after a meal at the in-laws.

Bags were packed and we were ready to go. I'm sure you know how these stories go, so I don't feel the need to continue with it. However I will tell you, I was one of the last people in the delivery room to hold my daughter; my beloved mother in-law knew about the water breakage prior to me. Better yet, she ever-so-kindly moved in to my house for over a week. I was unseen, and that's the best feeling in the world. All I wanted was to be a daddy. It sucks when you are physically present, but no one acknowledges your presence. Families are wonderful, at least that one is.

Needless to say, a few months later, my wife packed our home completely up with the loving and caring help of her mother and father, two brothers, and one uncle, leaving for

Bum F*ck, Egypt. I do miss that pretty black truck and all my furniture! That truck had a brand-new sound system in it. I had just put it in a couple weeks before the arrival of our baby girl.

A guy goes through his share of feelings, as well, while his little one is on the way. Contrary to popular belief, women are not the only ones with emotions. Even scientifically, it's goofy; a month back I had to undergo an Alcohol/ Substance Abuse Evaluation for custody proceedings. Yup, she took me there too! I had got a DUI a couple years ago, and she tried to hold it against me in court. Andrew is not a fit father. Please! Stuff happens. Not justifying the damn thing, but you learn from those fun incidents.

Actually, I'd have to say, those three months in jail on work release were the best three months of our marriage. I got out of jail every day from seven to seven for work and was ordered to return to jail after work. Again, against popular belief, if used correctly, jail does not have to be a damper on one's sex life. We had sex more in those three months than in the entire five and a half years we were together.

I owned a lawn care business at the time, a very well-rounded business to boot. Things were moving along with the business a lot faster than I anticipated. I had one full-time employee. That guy had to have been the dumbest guy I had ever met. But when dumb and nice come together, they usually make a good pair. It was approaching five o'clock. I ended every day back in the office I leased to tie up any clerical and billing I might have. My wife brought me dinner every evening before I returned to jail and she usually brought something else the best piece of ass I think I've ever had.

She didn't do much with it, but it was good. On top of that, that woman could blow a golf ball through a garden hose in her sleep. Needless to say, that office was where my beautiful little girl was conceived, right on an authentic, multicolored, red Persian rug.

I got up, sat in the office chair, she still on the rug, still on her back, legs in the air. Confused, I said, what are you doing? She peered up over her ass and pulled the inside of her knees closer to her chest so she could see me. "It helps fertility." I forgot to mention, she was a schoolteacher. She tends to look up stupid stuff on the Internet all of the time. Apparently, the site she read it on was verified by Norton Anti-virus.

The D Word

So, who in their right mind actually plans a divorce? I couldn't name one person who plans it. In America, here are the statistics:

Age at marriage for those who divorce in America

Age	Women	Men
Under 20 years old	27.6%	11.7%
20 to 24 years old	36.6%	38.8%
25 to 29 years old	16.4%	22.3%
30 to 34 years old	8.5%	11.6%
35 to 39 years old	5.1%	6.5%

Those of you over thirty-nine appear to be in good shape. Face it. Nobody wants to start over, especially if you're over half way through your life. And I mean that, starting over stinks! Collectively, looking at this chart, you'd think I'm OK...well, apparently not. I had a 77.7 percent chance of not getting divorced, what the happened then? Is my luck really that bad? "It" was close thirty furthermore, she would turn thirty in a few months. She had an 83.7 percent chance at it. Heck, if you add that up, our chances totaled 161.4 percent. Well, mathematically, that's not right. Who ever invented the word *average* sucks! Still, though, our chances for success were over 75 percent. I've played Keno; I've won that game before, and I'm sure the chances there are not even close to the statistics above. All I can say about that; is that life is a bitch, and then you marry her mother.

Divorce statistics in America for marriage

Marriage	Divorce Statistics
First Marriage	50% of marriages end in divorce
Second Marriage	67% of marriages end in divorce
Third Marriage	73% of marriages end in divorce

Now this is interesting. So I told my attorney, "I'm gonna get my nuts cut off and never marry ever again."

He said, "Please Andrew. Every one of my clients says that." Well, look at the statistics here. If you think things are bad now, the future looks promising. Then, if you decide to actually stick to your guns and not get married again, you get screwed by the state. If you're with someone for a certain number years, usually seven, they consider you in a common-law marriage. Either way, they have you. Sounds like celibacy is the way to go. But that's just no fun.

That was Easy...

"It" took off to Bum F*ck, Egypt, right? Well, that was over one hundred, fifty miles away from my home. That made custody impossible. She took my daughter with her, of course. Yep, that precious little garbling baby, the love of my life.

Then "It" went and filed a bogus protection order. This bogus protection order stemmed from a night during our separation, where she called the police on me for a mere argument. The police were only at our marital home for nine minutes, according to the police log. They then coded the call from initially being a possible domestic violence call to a civil dispute. Consequently, they left, and I left to remedy the situation. In fact, they even gave me a ride to the apartment I had a short-term lease on during our separation.

I'd had a few drinks earlier that evening, and I told the police officers that I wanted to leave, but I refused to drive intoxicated. They cordially offered to give me a ride to my apartment. I took them up on this offer and went home. I was at my apartment within twenty minutes of their initial contact at our home.

It was rather late, the latter part of one in the morning. I went straight to sleep in my small four-hundred-square-foot studio apartment, lights out on a stinking futon. Let me tell you, if you're contemplating a separation, spend the extra fifty bucks and buy a real bed. Your back will kick your ass for months to come if you don't.

The next morning, I woke up and re-lived the situation in my mind. I was fairly heavily intoxicated that night, and I wanted the full scoop. I figured I pay *bookoo* tax dollars for those men in uniform. I picked up the phone, and there wasn't even a report on file. The officer who answered was getting frustrated at my probing questions. He finally said he had to go, though he did confirm the call was logged at that address; however, it was nullified and cleared out by the two officers who responded. This call I later had to subpoena for a hearing to validate my claim.

After the phone call with the disgruntled police officer about the incident, I called a friend to give me a ride to my truck, which I'd left outside the home. It was gone. The house was locked as I fumbled through my fifty thousand keys; I realized that my house key was missing. Wouldn't you know it! The house looked pretty bare from the windows.

I put two and two together. I saw the tire tracks in the driveway. Her parents have an Avalanche. I have...had ca Dodge Ram. Yup, they had indeed been there. Those people are old, but holy crap, my mother in-law can speed! She must have made it to our house in a time warp.

My buddy started to drive away. I had to chase him down the street, arms flailing to get him to stop. He did. I went back to my apartment and sulked all day. What does a guy do?

* * *

I forgot to mention I owned another business, which was active at the time. I had three full-timers. I bought an investment property, a foreclosure. I bought it with a ton of equity with the hopes of making a buck or two. That truck was my main mode of transportation, as well as my lifeline for the business. I was in the very middle of flipping a house. I had to notify the guys not to come in to work the next day, because I didn't know how I would get there. Please, I hate cabs. Cab drivers are rude. Then they complain about tips. Furthermore, can I really ask a cab driver to stop at Home Depot, while I run in and get a two-thousand-dollar will-call order of materials? That would have been funny, though. The cab drivers here can barely speak English. They just point at the dashboard where the cab fair is displayed and say, "Pay thees Amot."

I finally called my financial adviser. He's the best. If I can't smile, all I have to do is call him. I made a small withdrawal, which I didn't realize was the start of many to come. I found this rusted out 1999 GMC Sierra. I am still sure to this day that they have some sort of illegal car-stripping business somewhere on the premises of the lot I bought it from. It worked, ran, and didn't smoke, at least not too much.

Now I had that taken care of. Monday rolled around. I went to work as usual. My guys were always late, anywhere from one to four hours. Keep in mind, they always expected a full paycheck. I was a moron. Yeah, you're fine. Just go ahead and make up the hours in the evenings or weekends. I understand you have child support. I promise to take care of you. Who was taking care of me? That's life. If you give them the chance, they'll poke ya right in the pooper; mind, I say lube please! These guys still have my washer and dryer to this day. Lesson to be learned, never hire your friends. And never make a business commitment at the bar. It never pans out.

Around ten in the morning, one of my guys came to me and told me someone was at the door. "Holy Pickle-Sticks," I said. OK now, keep in mind, this was my first flip. I pulled a couple permits, but there was no way I could pull the most important ones. My electrical and plumbing was getting thrown in by a guy I had bought drinks for at the bar the night before. Do you seriously think that guy was a licensed journeyman? Maybe a journeyman when it came to traveling to local watering holes.

I answered the door, and the man introduced himself as a constable for the sheriff's office. Oh, *God, now what? How could anything seriously get worse, here?* "Sir, are you Mr. Amil

A. Zeebs?" I said, "Yes." "I have some paperwork for ya, Sir." I know what you're thinking; who is Amil?

That's me. We'll get to that later.

He pulled out a brand new piece of paper that looked like it had just come straight off the printer. I swear the ink would have smudged if I had smeared it. "Sir, you are being served with a protection order. I need your signature on the line to verify that I delivered this order to you. Oh and please date it, thank you."

Thank you for what? What did I do for you?

The allegations in this stupid protection order made OJ Simpson look like an angel if he purportedly did everything he denied. How did all this happen? Am I hallucinating? Weren't the police called that night? Didn't they clear the call as a civil dispute and promptly leave our house in nine minutes? They did, they did. Oh no, not only was this protection order on my wife, it was on behalf of my daughter who was only three-and-a-half months old.

Violating a protection order isn't something you'd want to mess around with. I have heard stories, horrible, disastrous stories. No fun. I immediately went in to protection mode. Self defense mode Per Se; immediately, I thought, *she's one hundred and fifty miles away and "It" wants a protection order. Like I'm seriously going to drive two and a half hours with a gun on my passenger seat and a bottle of Jack in one hand.* "It's" mother took my truck, and do you seriously think that piece of crap truck I bought would make it very far outside of town before it gave in, as well?

I would never have done that; sounds fun, though. I'm not like that at all. Something inside of me did tell me that she was going to file for divorce in Bum F*ck, Egypt. Yup, BFE (Bum F*ck, Egypt), the epitome of a small town. Furthermore, if she did that, I would lose all jurisdiction in the county I live. I would have to drive to Bum F*ck, Egypt, for every hearing. That's almost five hours round trip. If I file first I win that battle at least.

Therefore, I got in the truck and drove straight to the courthouse. Do you know what it's like filing for divorce? Man, it sucks. "Sir, I'll need $26.50 for the initial filing, as well as a cashier's check for $30.00 to have her served." That's it? $56.50? That was easy...

Amil

The next day, I went to work as usual. Once again, except this time there was a small sticky notice on my front storm door. "Please call the Midwest County Sheriff's Office to arrange a time..." A time for what? Another order?

The same guy came back out. "Hey, how are ya!"

Just dandy, how bout yourself? I'm sure this guy was close to retirement, and this was all he did, just drive his car around all day and deliver bad news. It takes a special kind of person to do that. I know I couldn't do it.

"Sir, I have another order I need you to sign." The Dissolution of Marriage between the Plaintiff: Mrs. "It" and the Defendant: Mr. Amil A. Zeebs. I hate seeing that name. No not hers. I don't enjoy it very much but I can stand it. I'm talking about my first name. I have gone by my middle name my entire life; my mom always called me Andrew. Little did "It" know that I had filed just yesterday. It appeared we had a venue fight on our hands. Venue means place of jurisdiction; I didn't really know that until now. When I heard *venue*, I always thought fun, fun, beer, poker, fun, pool, fun. Nope, venue really sucks. I then got in the phone book and called some attorneys. They all said to basically grab my ankles and kiss my ass goodbye; this was just the beginning. "If you'd like to schedule an appointment, I am available next week." I did and met with three of them.

Come on, I've heard you have to be very picky about which attorney you choose. They find everything out about you. I picked the most affordable and easiest to talk to, great guy, has a few kids, himself. He's got one of those voices that just calms a person down.

Now the gloves are on...the bout shall commence. The first battle was the protection order. That one was fairly easy and inexpensive. I wish they were all like that. The drive was two and a half hours. I hate driving farther than the gas station, let alone one hundred, fifty miles. My attention span is about as short as my dick. Relatively speaking, 7 or so inches has to be equivalent to at-least a half hour.

We got there and, of course, there "It" was. I hired an attorney out in Bum F*ck, Egypt, because it would have cost me ten times that amount to use mine here in town. Two hundred dollars per hour. The drive would have cost me a thousand dollars. This did not even include the hearing, which took forty-five minutes. Then, of course, attorneys always do their thing behind closed doors, in the chambers with the judge.

We had a woman judge, great! She probably got her ass kicked by an ex husband and then decided to get in to law school. That's my luck. I took the stand, and there she was, and my mother in-law in the benches far to the back, holding my now four-month-old daughter. Oh, and I forgot to mention, this was our anniversary! Wow, what a great anniversary! I always dreamed of spending an anniversary glaring at my soon-to-be ex-wife in a courtroom in Bum F*ck, Egypt. That has to be every married man's dream.

The judge asked me questions. "Are you Mr. Amil... Zeebs?" There goes that damn name again! It follows me everywhere.

"Yes Ma'am." So we went through each and every single allegation on the protection order. Fun, Fun. The one where I allegedly got angry and floored the accelerator of my beautiful black Dodge Ram Quad Cab Hemi, straight into the back end of her Pontiac Grand Prix. That had to have been the best allegation! That's a big truck. You'd think it would have at least left a small scratch on one of our vehicles. Not a one. Neither of our vehicles had ever been to the shop for any type of body or cosmetic work, either. Put two and two together. What do we have here?

Finally, we got to the biggest and worst allegation. I threw her to the ground, spit on her, kicked her, punched her, got naked, and threw my clothes at her. Then went to bed...Wow, how do you combat that? Well, going back to police reports, wait, sorry...I left a small tidbit out. I threatened to suffocate her in her sleep. OK, now that's felony assault on her and felony assault on my daughter, not to mention felony terroristic threats. The police, well...apparently they had more important things to handle that night. They came to our house and woke me up, questioned both of us, and left nine minutes later. Let's do some more math. Two plus two is what again?

The judge, well I could tell wasn't buying all of this hoopla. Finally, the judge says, "Mrs. 'It,' according to police records, everything said here today is hearsay. I see no reason why the minor child must be in this protection order.

However, if you wish it for yourself then I shall grant it. If you feel threatened by your husband, I cannot take that from you. The order shall be revised to reflect the minor child is not included.

All-righty, we won that one. I had to get that protection order lifted off my daughter. If it had stuck for any reason, I definitely wouldn't be able to see my precious little girl. The drive back home was a heck of a lot better than the drive to Bum F*ck, Egypt, to say the least.

Looky...Looky...Here

The next week flew by. I consumed my time in the house working with the guys. Then I started looking at my finances and the job completion...Where are we, here? Not done, that's for sure. I went and found a "real" job while they worked on my house, so I wouldn't have to keep pulling money out of my investments to facilitate the business.

I used to sell copiers and printers for a fortune 1000 company. I'm pretty good at it. If there was a need, I could sell a subscription of *Penthouse* to a Nun. I got in the phone book and put a suit on. I immediately got hired at what seemed to be a reputable company. Oh God, this is good! The owner and I had a beer for the interview. That's sales though. Employers want to get to know you. He brought me on as his sales manager. I had no sales representatives, though. How contrary is that? What was I managing?

It took me a week to talk him into bringing on a couple of sales representatives. If you have ever been in the sales world and been in business-to-business sales, you're really going to relate to me here. This company was thirty years old. The owner apparently had two offices but he ended up closing one down. This office, where I worked...well, let's just say it wasn't doing so hot, either. He had me doing everything from sales, customer service, human resources, bill collecting, and reports. Isn't that like at least three or more departments wrapped up into one?

The owner was insane! You could tell this guy had lived in that office at some point in the last thirty years. The bathroom had a full-size bathtub for crying out loud! There was a kitchen in the back with a dishwasher, stove, fridge, and more counter space than my sixteen-hundred-square-foot house! Not to mention his personal office was the size of Manhattan with a pull-out coach. Yup, let's do the math. The guy kept all of his clients on a Rolodex. I'm twenty-six; it's 2010; Bill gates invented a little program called Microsoft in 1984. My office computer was running Windows 95, not XP, Vista, NT, or even the new one. Even Windows XP has got to be close to ten years old now! We were running an operating system that was developed when I was eleven.

The guy wouldn't give me a list of his current customers. He said, "I had problems with that in the past. That's what shut my other office down. Some sales people took my customers to a competitive company." My team quota was $75,000.00. I had no marketing materials whatsoever to give out to potential clients. If this wasn't a job from hell, then tell me where I went wrong! This stupid job lasted about two months. I gave the owner an ultimatum. I said, "Please give me the tools I need to effectively run a productive sales force." He said no. I said, "OK. Well...I'm forced to resign."

I forgot to mention the house-flipping business I had running at that time, as well. One day I got off work and went to the house at five in the evening and found something.

So I used to buy the guys working at the house cases of bottled water and leave them in the refrigerator. Well one of the smart ones decided to cut the tops off and use the base as a potting mechanism. I always sent them to Home Depot to pick up orders of material for the house. Apparently, on one venture to Home Depot, they bought a bag of Miracle Grow. Now we had some authentic ingenuity coming together here. Needless to say, I never got that receipt. I walked down in to the basement and looked around. They never cleaned anything up at the end of the day. All of my tools were thrown everywhere. It kind of looked like they were playing flag football with my hammers and screwdrivers. I couldn't tell who won, though.

I stepped into the furnace room and BINGO, holy mother-of-God! Looky..looky...here! Fifteen marijuana plants neatly organized on a two-by-four, with a light shining about a foot or two directly on them. My jaw hit the floor. Manufacturing a controlled substance carries a penalty of up to twenty years in a state penitentiary. That's exactly what I wanted to do with the rest of my life! On top of that, there were fifteen of them. I think we're doing good at math now. That's somewhere around three hundred years in prison. My attorney had been to the house to take pictures. If he would have found that! Uh....Um...Well...Let me explain... You get the gist. I had a dumpster outside the house. I immediately, quicker than I react when my dick gets caught in my zipper, threw all of it away. I went to Home Depot that night and re-keyed the house. I then took all of the tools my employees had brought over and put everything on the enclosed porch. I sent a text message telling them not to bother coming in to work the next day; they didn't work for me any longer. Lastly, I said pick your tools up as soon as possible; they're located on the porch. Good luck!

I wish I could tell ya that I come up with this stuff. But it really does happen to me. Every once in a while, I run in to those guys at a local watering hole I go to. This sounds interesting, doesn't it? They hate my guts for firing them. I tried to explain my reasoning. They wouldn't hear it. Darn near started a fight. I have never really been in any fights, either. I'm not a fighter. I'm sure I can hold my own to some extent. I'm in decent shape. But fights are no fun. Someone always ends up hurt and you have to deal with the consequences a heck of a lot longer than if you had just walked away. Their rationale for the small farm they were cultivating in my basement was, "It's no big deal! They were all dead or dying. They were less than an inch or so in length." I bet the judge would have been fine with that as well! Judges understand. I'm sure nothing would have come of it, if the authorities had found them. Plus, I'm sure "It" would have had a ball with that one. There Andrew goes again; he's such a bad man!

"Mommy let's get Daddy a present for Father's Day."

So Father's Day was the weekend coming up. I got to the house to do some work, and the FedEx guy rapped on my storm door. I answered and signed for a package. What was this? I wasn't expecting anything from anyone. I didn't have any family. My mom died when I was eight; my grandparents had passed; my dad was a jerk and had never been there for me; and finally, I was an only child.

Sound's like a mess, but you learn how to live with it.

I grabbed a box cutter and then looked at the return address. Sure enough, it was in my soon-to-be ex-wife's handwriting. I tore into the box and, well…"It" sent me a Father's day gift from my five-month-old daughter. How sweet… Please, the woman skipped town, stole everything, from my truck to my daughter. Now she had the audacity to send me a gift. I'm sure my five-month-old daughter didn't just wake up and say, "Mommy let's get Daddy a present for Father's Day." Furthermore, I hadn't seen my daughter for over a month at that time. I had to wait for a court to order the visitation. "It" made it clear that she would not give her to me.

She sent me a picture of my baby, a small canvass with her hand prints, and a card. It appeared that she used my baby's hand to scribble, "I love you!" How sick and twisted was this? Send me a card and gift for Father's Day, while depriving me of visitation? I gave it all to my attorney. I pay the guy for a reason. Evidence, evidence, evidence. My attorney said, "Andrew, go get yourself a nice dinner tonight and relax. Her day is coming, hey uh...don't quit smoking, either."

I said, "I won't, thank you."

To be continued...

"Mommy let's get Daddy a present for Father's Day."

A divorce has the tendency to dislocate your mind from its natural state.

This entire entry is being composed in real-time. A very touching incident happened last night that I would love to elaborate on.

As I told you before, I wish I could tell you that I come up with this stuff. But it really does happen to me. Last night, I invited a friend over for a beer. We sat in my living room and drank a tall boy. It happened to be Labor Day weekend. I didn't have class the next day and proposed that he and I go duke it out on the pool table over a pitcher of beer. He accepted my challenge, and we went to the renowned watering hole I enjoy the most in my venue.

I grabbed my pool stick, and well, I made a commitment to myself to never step into my vehicle with even a drop of alcohol in my system. So, therefore, I gave him the keys to my BMW, which he so loves to sport.

We arrive and ordered a pitcher of Bud Lite. I happen to be partial to Jager-bombs, so that also helped commence a very interesting night. About an hour after I had lost about every game on the pool table, I looked at my friend and said, "Wow, look at her." I pointed inconspicuously over at a beautiful, short-haired, dirty blonde at the bar. "That's my wife, curves and all. Damn, she looks good, even her ass; it's one of those asses that are really nothing special until you get to know it." He smiled and we played another game of pool, which, consequently, I won. I shot horribly that night. I hate bringing my pool stick then not having the ability to use it to the best of my ability. Sure, I made a few decent shots; but a divorce has the tendency to dislocate your mind from its natural state.

I kept my eyes on this pretty little thing. She happened to be with one of my friend's wives. Purely out of curiosity, I walked up to my friend's wife. "Hey, how goes it tonight?" They all love me up there. The bartender always flirts and grabs my ass out of spite, at least once a night. She was old enough to be my mother, but I love flirting back. I'm not even close to being ready to date again. I'm not even divorced yet. I know there are a lot of people who start looking for their next victim during their separation, but that's not me. I can handle being single and lonely, at least for ten years, maybe more, if the opportunity presents itself.

My friend's wife said, "This is Marney. She's going through a nasty divorce and we're just out trying to make her smile." Bingo! My friend looked at me and smiled mischievously.

"Wow, I might be able to relate to you, there. Life's a bitch, then you find out you married her mother." Everyone smiled. I felt compelled to buy a round of shots. "Sherry, can I get four...no wait, five Blackhaus? Thanks, darlin'."

Sherry went to the cooler and grabbed the remedy to a painful, yet ironic, moment. "Cheers...to good people, bad sh*t, and hopefully better times to come!" I can't do those very often. They tend kick my ass. But it went down a lot smoother than I remembered.

I said to my friend, "Yep, a cigarette is in order." We stepped out. I studied Marney. Not because I wanted to pick up on her, simply because she intrigued me. I had not seen my wife up close for a solid four months. This was her, even down to the way she dressed, super conservative. I came to the realization that I am attracted to these kinds of women, and they are to me, as well. They look at me like their bad boy. I'm somewhat foul mouthed, if you haven't already guessed. I have a smile that would tear just about any woman's clothes off. Conservative women like Marney see a guy like me with a few tattoos and the ability to hold an intelligent conversation as an escape from the everyday norm.

I busted out a seventy-nine-cent purple lighter that made smoking a chore and finally lit up a Marlboro Smooth.

"Well, hi Marney! Sorry to hear about your misfortune. Is it a nasty split?"

"Yeah, a really nasty one. I have a protection order on him."

Just when I thought the night couldn't get anymore amusing, I said, "Wow! Those are no fun." My buddy's eyes fell to the back of his head, I think, partially because we had just downed two hard shots in less than twenty minutes. And, of course, my buddy knew about my clear and present danger.

I stood up, and Marney said, with a flirtatious smile, "Have a good night!" I returned the gesture. Needless to say, I didn't shoot pool very well the entire night.

Continued

So, as I said, I took all of this evidence to my attorney and asked him about Father's Day. This was my first Father's Day as a father and I told my attorney that I would be crushed if I couldn't at least spend some of it with my beautiful little girl. He said he'd see what he could do and to get a hold of him in the latter part of the afternoon for the verdict.

Well, of course, "It" didn't want to drive one hundred, fifty miles to bring her to me. So I had to do it the expensive way. I had the judge order it; consequently, it was the Friday, prior to Father's Day Sunday, at three o'clock in the afternoon. If that's not waiting until the last minute, then please tell me what is.

My attorney called me right after he left the courthouse. His voice was excited. "We did it! Not only did the judge order you get her for Father's Day but every Sunday thereafter, from twelve noon until six o'clock!" I was very happy. "And, furthermore, your wife has to drive and deliver your daughter to your doorstep." Wow! This had to be the best news in the world, at least in the last long grueling months!

Father's Day was great. As she was ordered, she promptly arrived at noon. OK, one thing. I hadn't seen this little girl for over two months. Every day is a new day to an infant. My four-month-old didn't even remember my face. Imagine this: you're placed in an excited person's arms in an unfamiliar place. That's scary. She cried like nobody's business. I had to flick on the plasma television to get her attention elsewhere and calm her down. I also had no toys and really no furnishings for her.

I think I maxed out the SD card on my digital camera. I did that just about every time she came to see me. That's horrible isn't it? Your four-month-old daughter has to come see you, not by choice but court order. As a father, a man should see his bundle of joy every single day. That disconnectedness distorts a person's mind like a tornado without warning signals blaring from the towers.

However, it was a start. Beginnings must happen at some point. I'm a firm believer that there is no wrong time for a positive beginning.

Honesty is not always the best policy when it comes to the court...

What was about to transpire was probably filmed on a *Doctor Phil* episode about a thousand fold. I called my attorney the next day to tell him about the visit. I was completely honest with him; his empathy was very much appreciated. I explained the visit from beginning to end.

She had taken two naps and I had fed her once. In between the naps and feeding, there was nothing but crying. I could not pacify her. She did not know me, and if any of you have kids, you're very familiar with "stranger danger."

Furthermore, I'm a brand new papa. The only time I had held a baby before this was when I was a child myself and had held newborn cousins. Don't get me wrong, before all the nasty stuff transpired between "It" and me, shortly after our baby was born, I held her quite a bit. But "It" had never even left me alone with her, longer than twenty-minute intervals to run to the store. So, having her for a long period by myself was overwhelming for both of us. I don't mean overwhelming to the point where I wanted to return her to her mother, but it was overwhelming to the point that I couldn't calm her down.

I didn't know any tricks of the trade; I explained this to my attorney. I then told him that the only way for me to learn them were more frequent visits. Since every day is brand new to an infant, only seeing her once per week would still make me a stranger in my daughter's eyes. He concurred and set a hearing in front of the judge. Honesty is not always the best policy when it comes to the court...

I was pimped out

I was working for that stupid company as a Sales Manager, at the time of the court hearing. I took half the day off, after threatening to quit, because my boss didn't seem to understand the importance of my being in court that day.

I took Dodge Street downtown to the courthouse. Dodge sucks. Everybody drives like a maniac on it, but it's the quickest route from my office. I hate parking downtown, too. I probably have a parking ticket from an expired meter somewhere floating around that I forgot to pay. This time, I knew this hearing would be somewhat lengthy, so I spent the extra seventy-five cents and pulled the Beamer in to the parking garage, versus the metered parking.

I sweated bullets walking into the courthouse. No, stupid, not because of the hearing! It had to have been one hundred and thirty degrees outside, and I was in a full suit; I could barely breathe. I had to use my tie to wipe the sweat from my brow. OK, maybe the hearing was a portion of the stress.

Holy mother of God, there "It" is sitting in the far back of the courtroom, I thought as I spied "It." I said to my attorney, "I didn't know she was going to be here!" Alone, too, that was strange. Usually, her so-caring mother graced me with her presence. Yay! I didn't have to swallow my vomit this time!

My attorney advised me on what he was going into the chambers to speak to the judge about. And seriously, her attorney just eyeballed me. I couldn't tell if she wanted me to grudge f*ck her or blow my head off with a .357. Probably both...I was pimped out in a snazzy suit.

My attorney said, "Go take a seat in the courtroom. I'll be back in a little bit to get you."

"What! I have to sit in the same room with the woman who basically castrated me in every way possible?"

"Just sit in the front. You don't have to look at her." That wasn't the problem. I *wanted* to look at her. I love her. I don't want to be here going through this. Don't get me wrong. I brought it upon myself in some aspect. But you don't always bring on the things you want in life. Sometimes, you bring things on yourself that truly disgust you, kind of like a piece of rich cheesecake after eating a ten-course dinner at a steakhouse. You didn't do it because you wanted to, but rather felt obligated to.

She had forced me to take it to this level. I will not just shut up and go away. I'm pretty long-winded, and I always have to make my point clear. I just hate doing it through another person who costs me two hundred dollars an hour. I love my attorney, but attorneys know they're expensive. They have all the right to be. You wouldn't catch me going to law school and studying words written in a six-point font that are constantly getting changed because our congressional system can't make up their minds.

I sat two rows up from "It," directly in front of her. The annoying kind of in-front-of-someone, too, like when you're at the movie theater, and the guy in front of you has a melon the size of the moon. You're forced to look at the back of his head. I then stretched my arms out across the seat next to me, exposing the three-caret diamond wedding ring on my right hand, which so boldly had both of our initials and wedding date engraved on the inside. Yeah, I went through a phase where I tried to wear it as a cocktail ring; that didn't last very long.

My attorney stepped out and called me out the door. His face was hard to read. My only question, "Did we win?"

He said, "This is what the judge ordered. You need to complete a parenting class, go to counseling, get a full-fledged psychological evaluation, then get a substance-abuse and dependency evaluation, and then you get to see your daughter every Wednesday in Bum F*ck, Egypt, from seven to eight in the evening, under the supervision of a qualified person. Every Saturday and Sunday, 'It' is required to bring her to you at your apartment, from twelve to two and Sunday, from two to four, under the direct supervision of a licensed mental health practitioner (LMHP) one day, and a qualified person the next."

"Uh...uh...OK...Where do I start?" "No, you must not have heard me. We won. She has to drive seven hundred, fifty miles a week or she's in contempt of court."

I said, "Wasn't this on Oprah last week?"

He smiled. "I'll get you the phone numbers of the organizations to contact regarding these orders."

I lost about ten pounds in water weight through sweat; that hearing baffled me. I spent the entire next week getting everything set up. Can we say expensive? I called the place my attorney told me to for the psychological evaluation, and the receptionist proudly boasted, "We'll see you Tuesday, and don't forget to bring that fifteen hundred dollars when you check in!" I called the place for the alcohol and substance abuse evaluation, and that gal said,

"Wonderful, you're appointment is Wednesday and you'll be expected to pay five hundred when you arrive!" I forgot to mention, I just gave my attorney fifteen hundred yesterday. I also found out that we had used up all of those monies for this part of the litigation process.

Hopefully, my financial adviser answers and has something uplifting to make me smile. (He's the best...I told you, the first of many withdrawals to come!)

I hate going to Wal-Mart

The requisites were not as easy as one might think. In fact, how many people do you know that have had to go through these type of strenuous endeavors, just to spend a mere five hours a week with their little one?

Well, if you don't know anyone, you just met him. Hi! To say the least, everything the so-honorable judge ordered is either completed or scheduled for completion with many letters of satisfaction from the best in the industry.

The first visit on this schedule was an interesting one. "It" is really using that protection order on me as a leverage tool to back up. However, where there's a will, there's a way. I found out that I was not even supposed to step foot outside my own apartment when she was present in the parking lot.

In fact, prior to knowing this, I stepped out and went down the three flights of stairs to return my daughter to her mother (actually, my mother in-law). She was the receiving party while "It" was in the vehicle, protected by the ever-so-dark window tint that I so kindly did as a Christmas present less than six months before. You got it; it was like the presidential caravan. The door opened ever so quickly and closed ever so tightly, enough to make sure that eye contact would not be made.

There might have been a world-devastating earthquake if we had made eye contact. The woman had put me through the ringer ten fold. I couldn't blame her for not wanting to look at me, either. Come on, would you seriously want to look a person in the eyes while holding his testicles in your right hand and a severely dull bloody knife in the other?

This is where it gets fun. So my supervisor, bless her heart, followed me down the stairs. Oh my, and I'm glad she did. As soon as my mother in-law saw me coming down the stairs, she screamed bloody murder. Sounded something like stepping on Doug's tail! "NO...'It' is in the car! You need to go right back up the stairs!" OK, well, she didn't say "It," but she sure did say the rest. I truly hate this woman, my mother in-law. She's the proprietor of all evil things transpired and yet to be told. For all of you mother in-laws out there who think you need to act like Super Mother In-Law and protect your grown daughters without proper reasoning, besides your own: "Back-off!"

The next day came around and my attorney called me about the same time my alarm went off to go to work in the morning. "Andrew...what the happened this weekend?" Keep in mind, my attorney doesn't know me very well, yet. I had just hired him less than a month ago. Attorneys are the most...well, are *supposed* to be unbiased professionals, when it comes to cases. He is very unbiased, so he knows exactly who's giving it to him straight versus who's feeding him full of sh*t, wrapped in used toilet paper.

"Nothing, why?"

Well he said, "Her attorney is alleging you violated the protection order by running, cussing, swearing, and beating on "Its" car window."

Oh dear Lord baby Jesus! "No!" I did not do that! All I did was tell my mother in-law to calm down. "I'm home; if I wish to see my daughter off, I will!" I then told him to call the supervisor that witnessed the entire drama of passing off my daughter to verify the accuracy of my claim. He did, and she did tell him that everything I said was true. I'm thinking about changing professions...a professional golfer/hit man...

This is a diagram I had to make for court to prove that I was not even close to "Its" car. The ever-so-kind woman who facilitated the visits, well, I'm guessing got freaked out because she never answered my phone calls from that point on. Do you know how hard it is to find someone to give you every weekend afternoon to "Supervise" a visit? Look in the phone book; it's not like there's a category for Qualified Child Supervisors. I'm sure if there were, it would be a heavily used one by fathers like me.

Finally, I was ordered to drive to Bum F*ck, Egypt, to visit with my daughter for an hour. What? Bum F*ck, Egypt? Where is that? Wow! I Map Quested it.

Sure enough, it's a hundred miles! That's almost two hours, especially with traffic during rush hour. Getting out of the city I live in during rush hour is like trying to get a response from a statue; it's just not going to happen very quickly without a hammer and chisel.

Rush hour traffic is about as slow as my Internet connection.

Let me get this straight. She moves one hundred, fifty miles away from me with our daughter, and it's my fault... enough to have me drive two hundred miles a week. I told you, I hate driving. I hate going to Wal-Mart, too. But driving is at the top of my list. As you ordered, my so-honorable judge, I will drive a total of four hours round trip to spend one hour with my precious sweetheart.

* * *

The drive there always sucks: jerks in traffic, sitting for a long time, and having to listen to horrid radio stations because mine won't work halfway through the drive, due to loss of signal. Then, once I got there for the appointment, not only did the drive suck, but now I had to listen to this supervisor who was just like my mother in-law. "Andrew, it's OK...there are a lot of men out there who are just not good fathers."

What! Where was she getting this from? Directly from the cow's butt hole, that's where! "It" was the one to facilitate this, per the so-honorable judge. But I'm sure this supervisor wasn't fed these type of cow pies from "It," rather from my mother in-law. So needless to say, ignoring her wouldn't even shut the woman up. I tried; it just didn't work. What really sucks was that the visit was on the floor of this woman's office. Come on, when's the last time you vacuumed the floor? You expect me to sit my pure, untainted darling baby on that?

Please, she'll be just fine right on my lap. And no...I don't want your advice on parenting. I don't care about how many kids you've raised. Leave me alone and let me enjoy the miniscule sixty minutes I get with her on Wednesdays.

Thank you; here's fifteen bucks.

I'm also ordered to take parenting classes. Well they are on Wednesdays, the same time my only weekday visit is in Bum F*ck, Egypt. Try juggling that and let me know how it turns out. I'm supposed to be in two places at the same time. How does that work?

These classes are a joke. I'm the oldest person in the room. There's fifteen of us, ages ranging from fourteen to me, twenty-six. The kids wouldn't shut up either. They were bouncing off the walls. The instructor however was gorgeous. (When I mention gorgeous, that doesn't mean I tried to get in her panties. I'm simply recognizing beauty when I see it.) She's about "Its" height, and around her weight too, very petite...about five-foot-five and 125 lbs. She was wearing a pair of skintight, brown dress slacks. "It" has the exact same pair. I looked her over and what did we have here! Ms. Camel Toe, longtime no see! There was a young punk black kid with a house arrest band around his ankle that wouldn't stop beeping the entire two-hour session. The girl to my right looked over eighteen, but I glanced at her intake form and saw she was only sixteen. The instructor then made everyone do introductions. "I'm Andrew...I have a baby girl about seven months old." I left it at that. The next one started her introduction, and I knew the rest of this class would be long and very painful.

Ms. Camel Toe then had everyone stand up. The class consisted of mainly women. I made the comment after walking in. "Is this class gender biased?" I didn't know, but then another guy walked in, except he was with his girl-friend. Ms. Camel Toe had two people on opposite sides of the room holding cards, which defined emotions. She then asked everyone to move to the side of the room that best described how they felt, based upon the question. The first question was, "Did you plan your pregnancy?" Really? The sixteen-year-old girl right next to me immediately ran to the corner that said "Yes, it was planned." I then had to ask myself quietly in my twisted mind, "Why am I here... again?" Yup, for my precious garbling baby. I will survive. I love you, little girl!

The Eyes of "It"

The weekend visits are great! We have so much fun. To actually prove this to the courts, I video-recorded one visit. I got footage of everything from playtime, feeding, and nap time. In one part, I actually took my daughter's hand and addressed the court with her smiling. In a child-like tone I said, "Hi, everyone! Hi, Mommy; hi, Daddy; hi, Judge; hi, Attorneys! We really are very appreciative you let us spend time together!"

I was told many a time, but never truly understood the magnitude of it, until I found it slapping me right on the chin, "From birth, a mother has fifty-one percent rights. That extra two percent is usually the ultimate deciding factor on if, when, where, and finally how often a father can see his child if the two split up."

I'd really have to say the worst part about it is that I don't want to split up from my wife. I do love her, and I still love her with all of my heart, as much as I did when I put that small diamond on her finger while eating Chinese one evening after coming home from work. That's a funny story in itself. Our favorite place to get Chinese was this hole-in-the-wall not far from the ghetto. They knew our faces and gave us that Chinese, squint-eyed grin every time we went in there. I came up with the novel idea of putting the engagement ring inside a fortune cookie. I went through about twenty before I got it in one without destroying the cookie. I had printed a small strip of paper comparable to that of a fortune that read, "Will you marry me?" and stuffed that in, resealed the plastic with a lighter, and put it on top of her portion of fried rice in a Styrofoam container.

I got home from work and was tired as usual. I told her I didn't feel like cooking tonight and just picked us up Chinese for dinner. She loved Chinese. I got her favorite sweet and sour chicken with fried rice and crab ragoon. I highly doubt I'll eat that anytime soon, consequently. I plopped the bag of food on the dining room table and took a seat. She gave me a kiss (always a short peck), then opened the bag. "What did you get us?"

I said, "Here's yours, babe, sweet and sour chicken as always." That's actually my favorite, but I hated getting the same thing as her, so I usually tried to switch things up a bit and get a broccoli and beef or something. We ate, and I sweated nails the entire dinner. She ate so damn slowly, and I couldn't take my eyes off that fortune cookie. I might have to stop there. I'd hate to short my keyboard out with tears.

I guess things happen for a reason. What's horrible is that, in a divorce, memories are always cashed aside. I only get a glance at "It" on weekends, for a short forty-five seconds, as she gives my daughter to the supervisor I hired for the afternoon. Post pregnancy takes its toll on some women, but not her. She's always as glowing as I remembered, waiting for her to walk down the aisle. Soul mates I do believe only come once in a person's life, and I do believe she was mine. There I go again. Let's finish the conversation about the visits, because now, that's what this is all about: a father's drive to fulfill his commitment to his daughter through thick and thin.

I had actually got the protection order modified to let me text message "It" regarding our daughter. Before this, I had to go through her dreadful mother. That woman actually filed for divorce against her husband, whom she's been married to now for over thirty years. He got on his hands and knees, I guess, and well, there was no second or third-party intervening them protesting it; and they made up. So I'm sure she's indirectly taking this out on me through her daughter to this day.

"It" and I text each other regarding visitation, health, well-being, and other parenting related matters. I have to be very careful in what I say. Because if she got the nerve, all she would have to do is contact my city's police department, and I would be arrested quicker than my cat Doug eats a piece of pizza. And let me tell you, that cat eats things that would amaze you!

She refuses to tell me where our daughter is living, moreover even where she goes to daycare, for crying out loud. I'm ordered to pay forty-two percent of those costs, as well, per our so-honorable judge. On one occasion when she dropped off our daughter for a visit, she put a list of daycare receipts in her diaper bag. I studied them. The initials matched that, coincidentally, of her sister in-law's initials, who is voluntarily unemployed and stays at home all day with her two children. The irony kills me. This sister in-law even told me prior to the sh*t hitting the fan that if we moved out there, she would gladly watch our daughter, basically free of charge or damn near close to it. These receipts were those of an Office Depot, very generic and basic. I'm guessing the receipt book cost in the realm of twenty dollars on a high note. Put two and two together here once more for me, please!

My supervisor gets my daughter from her mother's arms and brings her to mine. It seems as if every time I get her, she just ate, and so our visits are very limited to one half-hour of play, about one hour of nap-time, and then she'll wake up when I'm organizing her toys and belongings one half-hour before her departure. This is OK. This is about her and her only. I sometimes watch her sleep. I can see so much of her mother in her. Hopefully, she'll get more of my traits as time progresses, but for now, I'm forced to watch the eyes of "It" rest ever so softly in a crib in my spare bedroom which, consequently, is only occupied a few hours a week.

Now I'm seeing her three days per week, but only two times for two hours at a time on weekends and once on Wednesday for an hour. My good friend goes with me on the long drive to Bum F*ck, Egypt, to keep me company. He's a hoot, but life takes an interesting evaluation when such a devastating and traumatic event like this so kindly happens to pop its head in the door. That's when you truly find out who your friends are. We were on the way back home after a visit in Bum F*ck, Egypt, and my buddy said, "Yup, she knows who Daddy is." Those had to have been the kindest words I think I had heard in months.

Every day is a new day to a baby, so my biggest priority was leaving her with a strong fatherly impression. Fortunately, and strangely enough, with such limited visitation it has worked. The little girl falls asleep in my arms within as much comfort as a pillow-top mattress. She hates it when I set her down to grab something from the other room. She's content in my lap, taking her little tiny fingers through the hair on my arms. And let me tell you, I'm one hairy beast; the hair on my arms is longer than her precious fingers.

Man those little ones have a grip from hell, too! The little girl gets a hold of my chest hair every once in a while and puts me in an unrelenting death grip.

Love is something a person truly does not understand, until one of these precious darlings comes into their life.

Toilet Paper!

I've come to the understanding that divorce has a tendency to make or break someone. Look at the bar scene. More than half are divorced. I don't mean the bar on a Friday or Saturday night, rather late nights, during the week. It messes with your mind to the point that all you want to do is get away from yourself. I'm doing my best to keep so busy that just doesn't happen.

For starters, I'm writing this book. Secondly, I'm back in college going full time. I'm taking fifteen credit hours. I don't think you heard me...*fifteen* credit hours. I'm no spring chicken; that's a whole lot of studying. I truthfully hadn't picked up a book since I went to jail/work release about two years ago! I have to force myself to keep up. It keeps me busy, though. Thirdly, I'm still renovating my house, which is presently on the market. Yup, the same one I bought to ultimately flip!

You're probably thinking, where does this guy get time to write a book? Got me! It keeps me busy, I guess. The following Sunday was a rather eventful day and rather humorous to boot!

I woke up at eleven in the morning. I had to throw "in the morning" in there. I sure didn't want you to think I slept all day. I have to sleep in occasionally. "It" once told me that I'm just like a little kid. I wear myself down to the point where my body shuts down and says...night...night.

I flew out of bed, well the couch. Not even a couch, a love seat. My realtor said my couch was too big for the living room, so it had to go. I fell asleep watching a movie last night and, well, the love seat was the spot. I do have a large ottoman that helped the cause. I promptly got dressed. I then prioritized what little day I had left. My little one would be here that afternoon, so I had three hours. Three hours is a lifetime to me. I can get a whole heck of a lot done in three hours. I learned years ago that it's not necessarily how much time you have; rather, it's what you spend your time doing that counts.

I needed to get my haircut, get a new pair of shoes, change the oil in the Beamer, visit with my daughter, go pick up my washer and dryer, do laundry (mind, I say hook up the washer and dry), run to Wal-Mart and get groceries, mow the lawn, and lastly, do an assignment from a class I'm taking. Holy crap, all in three hours? How was this going to work?

Let's prioritize this. What needs to get done during business hours while stores are open? Haircut, shoes, Wal-Mart...no, wait, they leave it open for tweakers twenty-four-seven. Let's just say I had a rather eventful day and, of course, I forgot one thing ...toilet paper!

God, I hate my mother in-law!

I've been working on my credit during this divorce. I finally am getting it real close to a rating of seven hundred! So I own my house outright and decided to pull a very small home equity loan out of it to pay my attorney's last bill. That sounds easy, but it's not. I spent hours upon hours on the phone with lenders, "Well, Sir...you have a very limited credit history." Excuse me? Seriously? I own the house outright, and furthermore, all I want to do is pull not even a tenth of what it's worth. Less than ten thousand. I'm leaving over ninety-percent equity in it and you won't touch it?

When people say that your house is your investment, tell them to look at the market. Especially in today's market. You'd be better off buying a sand hut in a third-world country. On top of that, we have our first black president who says he's fixing the economy and just spends money we don't have. We are trillions of dollars more in debt, and the Dow Jones isn't even close to fourteen thousand points, as it was not long ago. The unemployment rate is almost higher in percentage than the sugar in this ice-cold, cherry-Pepsi that I am drinking. Mr. President, I am waiting for your so-called "Change," and it looks like you have a couple of years left. Don't bail out any more companies! I could have used some relief paying for my divorce and custody battle, and it would have been way more productive than the bailouts you did not so long ago.

I read last week about the bill passed by the local mayor here in my town, and we are going to pay more in taxes! It makes no sense to me whatsoever? Property taxes are going to go up 2.5 percent, as well as restaurant and bar taxes? They're also going to charge a commuter tax for anyone who lives outside of town and drives in to go to work! How ass-backwards is that? It really makes a person just want to hide all of their income from Uncle Sam and work under the table. No wonder why we are "the richest country in the world" or close to it. Uncle Sam educates us, we get jobs, he taxes us to death and back, then he uses that money to save banks and financial institutions that can't make it on their own? "Yeah sure! We'll pay you back," then they all go into chapter 11? It makes a whole lot of sense to me; I'm sure Uncle Sam is going to send us all fat-ass checks when these companies pay him back. So, make sure to check your mailbox every day!

That tax hike generated over $30,000,000.00 for my city! The mayor so proudly boasted, "We're going to use that money to help the hurting police and firefighter retirement plans and fix our roads." I didn't mention they just built a multimillion-dollar baseball stadium, because the old one where the college world series has been held every year "Isn't Good Enough." Lord, that thing's been there longer than I've been alive, and it's done just fine. They just laid off over a thousand elementary and high school teachers, here, as well as in the surrounding areas. Yup, we need a brand new baseball stadium!

Enough political science. I finally found someone... some bank to give me the loan. "Sir, we need your wife's signature on the deed of trust." What! Why do you need her signature? "Sir, you were married when you bought that property, even though you were legally separated and it is solely in your name." Holy mother of God, do you really think she's just going to hop, skip, and merrily jump right down to the bank and sign that lovely piece of paper?

I called my attorney and gave him the scoop. I further explained that I had bought the house with non-marital funds. I even went down to my broker's office and got the paper trail, including my bank receipts. He took all this to her attorney, but she refused to sign it. She said, "I have marital interest in that house. I'll sign it, though, if he gives me $10,000." Huh? Marital interest in what? No way. This is an easy one.

Well, we go to court on a motion to compel. Basically, the judge would just make her sign it. It was a Wednesday and I had a visit in Bum F*ck, Egypt, that evening and court was at three o'clock. She somehow managed to dig up a Wells Fargo Bank statement from last year that showed we had nineteen thousand in a cash money-market account. Well, I kept my finances from her, and she knew this. So she probed. She always made me nervous about that.

I inherited a nice chunk of change a few years ago, right after I got it, "It" said, "Why don't you put me on that account?"

I told her, "Honey I can't. It's an FBO (for the benefit of) account. You can't modify who's on it." Legally you can't without cashing it out and paying dear Uncle Sam. Holy crap, I would have been shut down due to lack of funds if I somehow did that. That ten grand, however, came from the lawn-care business I had also started with non-marital funds, and on which I eventually took a small paper loss, according to the IRS. Well, I took twenty of the sale of the business and said, "Honey, let's buy a house with this when we sell this one?" Yay! Ya, right. For approximately three months, she talked me into putting the money in to a joint money-market account at the same brokerage I still use. I commingled the money! The best part is that I didn't even know it!

"It" is about as street smart as Mr. Rogers; this was her mother, my mother in-law, who came up with the brilliant idea to legally extort half of the nineteen thousand from me. Let me tell you, honestly, I was going to use that money as a down payment on our next house. But legally, it was all mine. She had no ties to my business (she wanted nothing to do with it when I first started it). I started the business with non-marital funds and then showed a paper loss to the IRS. So, if I had profit, she would have been entitled to that; however, I did not. But since I put the money into a joint account for even a day, it was considered commingled! Lesson learned!

She was trying to say I had used that money on the house I bought to flip, which I did not. This was either going to cost me nine thousand, five hundred, now, or nine thousand, five hundred in the future. I am a firm believer in paying now if you have it. I did, and she signed a non-interest clause on my house and, well, "It" got nine thousand, five hundred dollars out of me.

Here's an interesting twist to the story, I was never on the house that she owned. However, I made half of the mortgage payments for the three years of our marriage living in it. Therefore, it is a marital asset. I am entitled to half of the equity for the three years we were married and lived in it together. I really don't want it. But my mother in-law is making me take this to the next level! I don't want to hurt "It." I love "It." "It" is the mother of my precious garbling baby. "It" is/was my soul mate. God, I hate my mother in-law!

I'm thinking about starting a happy fan club. Wanna join?

Better yet, I returned home from my last class. Math. I hate math. The only thing I like about it is looking at the student instructor. Every time I leave that class, I have a migraine beating on the inside of my brain. Seriously, I've been so confused during class that I have had to attend an average of two quiet studies in the mathematics laboratory, on top of my normal class schedule. We had a test today. You'd think that it would be easy, since it was only eleven questions. Not a chance! I barely got done in time. Good thing it was multiple choice; otherwise, I would have been better off putting hieroglyphics in place of the answers.

I checked my email after giving up on hooking up my washer and dryer. Yup, that was supposed to get done the other day, and I still haven't washed clothes. Good thing I have a couple bottles of body deodorant; otherwise, I'm sure I'd have some pleasant comments come my way. NCS, Online billing statement...What is this? My Internet is slower than than two old people screwing, so while it was loading, I had time to turn on the radio and grab a soda. When I returned, I found that the Child Support Center sent me an invoice. I pay $483.00 a month and only get to see my daughter twenty hours a month. That breaks down to $24.15 per hour. I'm really not very good at math.

I'm only good with quick add ups and division, which that is. It's enough to make a guy gag.

Since I'm a full-time student, I really don't have any income, either. I'm living on Stafford loans at an interest rate that would probably make me gag, too, if I knew it. This was calculated based on that stupid-ass job I had as a Sales Manager for a period of only two months. Courts are so caring and thorough when coming up with these numbers, though, we should all feel blessed that our legislature is truly taking care of every mother out there. Think about it. Child support is supposed to be half of what it costs to care for a child. They're telling me it cost almost $1000.00 per month, if you take my figure times two for "Its" portion of one child. That doesn't even include daycare, which I'm ordered to pay 42 percent of and a healthy portion of her health insurance. I'm not complaining about paying to take care of my daughter. I am, however, frustrated about the fact that it does not cost over $1,000.00 per month to care for one child. Let me raise our child, oh-so-honorable judge. Realistically, with all expenses included, it's probably about $600.00 to $700.00, dependent on the daycare involved. Remember those bogus daycare receipts that "It" pulled out of "Its" ass? Well, I've been thinking about giving her sister in-law a hefty raise for watching our baby, when my soon-to-be ex-wife is either at work or working on her next victim. I haven't come up with a dollar amount though...

If you haven't already guessed, this situation has made me the happiest person in the world. I'm thinking about starting a happy fan club. Wanna join?

Dear Beloved "It"

So I told you, I really didn't want this divorce to begin with, right? I am as steadfast in this position as a bull waiting to pummel the matador. I figured I would give it one last shot.

I have my reasons for being angry about the entire situation, but anger sucks. It has never solved one issue in this world. I wrote this letter and emailed it to my attorney praying to get it in the hands of my soon-to-be ex-wife. Take a look:

Dear Beloved "It,"
There is so much to say, but I will put it down in my perspective. I ask you to read this, then immediately look in the mirror:

I take Andrew to be my husband, to have and to hold from this day forward, **for better or for worse**, for **richer, for poorer**, in **sickness and in health**, to **love and to cherish**, from this day forward, **until death us do part**.

Nowhere in there did God say because my mother does not like my husband, it is OK to divorce him. We took vows and I meant them. The only reason I am the plaintiff in this divorce, which is not finalized, yet, is because I knew that your mother would back you ten fold with even the slightest thought of divorcing me. Which, consequently, she did, although it was a day late.

I filed as soon as I was served with that protection order, only because I knew that I would face a losing battle in Bum F*ck, Egypt, fighting to remain our daughter's father. Don't get me wrong. This has been severely expensive. I am worth approximately $40,000 less than I was six months ago. But money is not love.

I will always be her father, and I will always be right by her side. That will never change, even if these proceedings finalize in the direction they are heading. You know I have absolutely zero family, due to death, greed, dislocation, or severe animosity. I understand what it is like not knowing the man who brought you into this world. I will not let our daughter grow up with those forever-scarring pains. I'm twenty-six, and it still hurts, so imagine when our daughter is twenty-six. Time goes by so fast.

I know you love me. I also know that I was not the best husband. But as that verse ever so bluntly puts it, "for better or for worse." We need to save this marriage, because we are disappointing God. **We are in a sin that can be stopped.** Probably the worst sin of our lives. We can make this work. I will climb the tallest mountain in the world and die climbing it, if that's what it takes. Which means that I am already planning on moving to Bum F*ck, Egypt when my semester is up in December and transferring colleges, only for the sole purpose of being closer to our daughter. "It," I know no one in that town, but love will take care of me and, I pray, us.

If you truly meant those vows you made to me, you will reconcile with me in a fashion that is comfortable and pleasing to both of us, so that we may continue with our marriage and have more beautiful children and become grandparents ourselves. This is going to take work on both of our ends, but a vow is a vow. I have some work to do as a husband, which I understand and am willing to do, and you have some work to do as a wife, if you wish to remain committed to the vow you made to me and God.

I ask you to please make this decision on your own, without the interference from your family, whatsoever. I will respect your decision, and all I ask for in return is that you respect my role as our daughter's father. Please re-read the vows at the top of this page and return your answer to me, ever so kindly.

With Love, Me

Needless to say, I called my attorney and he said that there was no legal way to get this letter to her. That bogus protection order would throw me in jail quicker than all get out. Who knows...Maybe I'll send "It" a copy of the book from an anonymous donor. Wait, I can't do that; then "It" will know what's truly on my broken...twisted mind! God, I hate my mother in-law!

The Brady Bunch reunited. Let's party!

"You cannot give that letter to her, Andrew. Any contact, directly or indirectly, is a violation of the protection order, if it is not solely about your daughter." Again, in-laws are great! Families are wonderful, at least that one is. They've made damn sure we don't have any contact with the disgusting infiltration of "Its" mind.

"Oh, honey, you don't need him. You'll eventually meet someone who treats you better and is a great father to (your) daughter. And I, as your mother, will make sure of that."

"It's" mother took my wife and daughter right out of town and stuck them in her basement. Basically, right in her estranged husband's man cave. I'm sure he was happy about that moment. That guy is one of the neatest men I know. The guy drives a Harley with an engine big enough to fly an airplane. I feel kind of bad for the guy. She tells him what to do in basically every way possible. They must have a treaty of some sort comparable to the Treaty of Paris where Napoleon was ultimately defeated. Napoleon is now retired, bless his heart. The man has a heart the size of Texas, a beard, and a ponytail that damn near hits his ass. Dear Napoleon, you will be missed.

My mother in-law saw fit to bring all of her grown kids home. They all wandered the country and ended up settling down with their spouses and bringing little ones in to the world. The first one was "Its" younger brother. I felt bad for the damn guy. He told me on many occasions that he hated Bum F*ck, Egypt. There was no opportunity for him there in his career. He found his love in either Washington or Oregon, I forget. He went and knocked her up prior to them getting married. And this story still kills even today. I said, "It...I think she's pregnant." I whispered this because we were at a holiday dinner with the entire "It" family. "No, Andrew!" she protested. But I knew differently. Come to find out, less than a month later, they announced a new arrival to the family. Quicker than, they went to the courthouse prior to their little one's arrival. I remember "It" went to their reception with her mother out of state. When "It" returned, she told me in an excitement that I've never seen from her before that her brother was moving to Bum F*ck, Egypt.

They were hurting for money and, well, let's just say mother would not let this happen. She put the two of them in a house twice the size of ours. Then she even paid their mortgage for quite a while. She dropped almost $40,000 on the down payment for them. Well, when "It" found out about this, she was really jealous of her younger brother, and mommy told her that if she did the same, she would do the same as well. Bring 'em home cowgirl! Next was "Its" older brother. I could never put a finger on this guy. He was really apprehensive and evasive about everything. I think he got picked on in school. Nice guy, though, and a very hard worker. They talked him in to moving to Bum F*ck, Egypt. I still don't know the whole story; they kept this one more hush-hush. He had a few bucks, though; however, I'm sure they dropped a pretty penny on getting him back home, too. And well, you've heard "Its" story! That has cost them a pretty penny, as well. "It" didn't have much money when we parted. So mommy bought her that attorney who wanted to grudge f*ck me in the courtroom, that or watch me blow my head off with a .357. Mommy also landed her a job working for the local school district, immediately after she arrived in town. Now "It" is bringing in the most money she has ever made in her life, somewhere around $40,000 per year. Single and with "Its" lifestyle, she's sure to save up a fortune very quickly.

The funny part is that they all live about a mile or so from each other, all except "Its" older brother. He lives in a very remote part of Bum F*ck, Egypt, a little suburb right outside of B.F. E.. It's within ten or so miles, though. The Brady Bunch reunited. Let's party!

Every person in the world wants to hear those words!

This is a fun conversation. So I told you I went back to school. Holy crap! They don't call it school because it's easy! On top of that, I'm about the oldest person in all of my classes. The professor in my religion class was doing a lecture and popped an open-ended question. Are any of you in here over twenty-five? I damn near raised my hand. Grandma up front sure did, eagerly. I'm in a class of one hundred, twenty-plus students and only one student is over twenty-five? Well, two, if I would have honestly raised my hand. How does that work?

I transferred over a bunch of credits, so it's not my freshman year. I'm somewhere between my sophomore and junior year, in fact. I did however hate general education credits. So my academic adviser made me take those this semester. I'm in class with high school students. These kids are barely eighteen, all college freshman. I was waiting in line to get into class, and one kid struck up a conversation up with me. "You're older. How old are you?" Let me tell you, every person in the world wants to hear those words! So as anyone else, I figured, let him guess. "What about forty?"

No way! "Forty!" I said. "I'm twenty-six!" I'm in my prime; don't go there with me, son!

High school kids are funny. I call them high school kids because they were high school seniors within the year.

Their mentalities have not moved from that level yet. I was in religion at eight o'clock in the morning, and I was the only person drinking coffee out of over one hundred, twenty students. The professor put a movie on for half the class. I tend to like the back of the lecture hall. My hearing is fine. This punk eighteen-year-old directly behind was gossiping about some teenage thing. I could barely hear the movie. I turned around. "Man, keep it down!" This punk had to be over four inches or so taller than me; these kids are big. I heard him tell his buddy how he'd love to beat me up. "Look at him, he doesn't know who he's dealing with," he said. Kids, kids, kids.

Have you ever seen the *Girls Gone Wild* movies? Well I haven't either, but I have seen the commercials late at night. I swear they all come from a dorm somewhere on this campus. I keep to myself. I'm too old for them to mingle or talk to. It's good for me. I'm not there to mingle and talk, just to finish my degree. I went through that stage once. It was fun. Needless to say, I am truly enjoying it, although I had a different upbringing than most; it's an experience that everyone should have.

Let me tell you about the student body. Damn it looks good, the young women of course. I have quite a trot from my classes and get exposed to a wide array of women on my journey. I look at these beautiful young women and just shake my head. "Darlin', if you only knew what was coming to you in the next five to ten years. Your ass will fall two to three inches closer to the Earth, your boobies will get tossed around by a little friend named gravity, and that smile...Well, your eyes and dimples will inherit shadows and lines, every time you use them." Ignorance is bliss.

"Adult assembly required"

I had a visit last night in Bum F*ck, Egypt. It was quite inter-esting to boot. The visit is usually held at a non-profit com-munity assistance center. It's kind of interesting, why do they need a community assistance center in a town with a population less than the fingers on my hand? The manager of the center has been the supervisor and agreed to do so, of course, with the assistance of a few dollars. She canceled last night, but I was not about to miss a visit with the love of my life, my precious garbling baby.

"It" text messaged me and told me that the alternate place for the visit was at a local McDonald's. Seriously, Mickey D's? What are we going to play with French fries and chicken strips off of the dollar menu? I replied when I got in to Bum F*ck, Egypt. I happened to see a Wal-Mart, one of the big super centers. Wal-Mart...Really, I thought Wal-Mart had a minimum population stipulation. Nope, they'd put a Wal-Mart in the Gobi Desert if they could. They just don't; it's probably a plumbing issue.

My buddy was with me. As I told you, I hate driving. Company on a long drive makes time pass so much easier. I sent "It" this text message. "We are in the very middle of the Wal-Mart parking lot; we are in my silver BMW 328is. My friend will get her from you and we will go shopping together." I know I didn't have to throw in BMW 328is.

But I did facetiously. "It" knew what kind of vehicle I had. "It" sent her to me with a diaper, wipe, and a small, thin baby sheet. That's about all "It" gives me when we exchange our daughter. I buy her toys, but do you really think "It" sends even one back for the visit? Nope, not usually! I haven't been keeping the toys at my home, because, for now at least, our baby is with her mother for all but the five hours a week I get with her.

My buddy and I walked in to Wal-Mart, with me holding the best gift I had ever received. I found a shopping cart with a baby carrier and started to put her in it. It looked disgusting, like some other kid died shitting himself and crying in it. I took the sheet "It" had supplied for the visit and put it on top of the child seat. I have never had the opportunity to walk around a store with my own baby. I'm sure everyone in the store thought my buddy and I were gay, too. Seriously, how often do you see two grown men with a baby in a shopping cart carousing Wal-Mart? Neither one of them have a wedding ring on. Yup, everyone gave us the gay gawk.

I went down an aisle with my daughter and noticed women eyeballing me. If another woman goes in to Wal-Mart with her baby, people don't give a second look, well, not unless she's got a nice rack or something. But when a man goes in to the store with his baby by himself, women keep an eye on him. I think women find it sexy in some strange way when they see a guy being a dad. I knew a few women that walked by wanted my digits. "Well, little girl, you might help Daddy in ways you have yet to imagine." For now, though, we're good. "Where's the toy aisle?" You can't expect someone to go to Wal-Mart and not buy anything, especially for an entire hour.

I bought my little one a ton of toys and gadgets to play with at my house. I spent a hundred bucks; that store is a virus. You can't walk in there and expect to stay on a budget; there's no way. We had fun, though, and, well, eight o'clock always comes too soon. Time to go, baby!

The next day I had guys coming over to carpet my basement. I had bought this Baby Einstein child seat to help with learning motor skills and standing.

Yeah, that's it in the picture. I poured a cup of coffee and lit a cigarette. The instruction manual was nineteen pages! I'm a man. Do you seriously think I read directions? No wonder why it was called Baby Einstein; it came in six hundred pieces. "Adult assembly required." They forgot to mention you need a Master's with a minor in plastic-toy assembly to put this thing together.

I was sure the guys down in the basement were done with the carpet before I put the damn thing together. Sixty bucks and it didn't even come with batteries? I'm about 70 percent sure I connected all the pieces together correctly. Then I find the last small plastic bag with little tiny blue plastic covers. What is this? I had to bust out the nineteen-page novel to figure out where they went. After an hour of careful analysis, I snapped them into place. This had to have been the first time I had ever put anything together without extra parts that I would have to throw away.

Thanks, Dad!

I was goofing around on the Internet and typed my last name in to the Google search bar. Guess what popped up? My dad. This guy is a hoot, a holler, and a mess, all bunched in to one person. I clicked it. It took me to a genealogy web page. That was interesting...What did we have here...? My dad was married and divorced three times? I'm twenty-six; you'd think I'd know, wouldn't you?

Ages twenty-four, twenty-nine, and thirty-one? Damn! That's sickly amazing! He was married three times in seven years? That's one busy guy! I wonder if I don't have siblings out there that I've never met? He and I have been distant my entire life. I had to beg him to come to my wedding. I have flown out to see him many different times over the last few years. I asked him to come to see me, once, for my wedding, and he threw a temper tantrum like my daughter in Wal-Mart when I stepped out of her sight. I finally talked to his girl-friend at the time, and she talked some sense in to him.

About a year after I got married, I flew down to see my dad. I should have known things would go awry. We were walking through an electronics store, and it was about a week before my twenty-fourth birthday. When you get older than eighteen or so, you really stop expecting birthday presents. He said in his deep, foreign voice, "Which one you like, son?"

"That's a nice one," I said, pointing to a fifty-inch plasma screen, displaying some sort of color show to emphasize the vivid picture.

"Sir, get that one wrapped up. We'll take it."

Huh? I was baffled. I said, "How am I taking that on an airplane?"

He ended up not getting it, but rather buying one where I lived for me to pick up as soon as I returned. "Thanks, Dad!" Now this is the funny part! That night, we got into a huge argument, and I about dropped the little foreign guy in the middle of a parking lot, right off the freeway. I told him to pull over and let me drive. He had way too much to drink that night and was swerving all over the freeway. I finally got him to pull over. I got out of the car and started screaming at him. He pissed me off. He could have killed us or someone else. He was damn lucky a cop hadn't seen him driving like a maniac. He got out the car and could barely stand up. He was ripped out of his mind. We'd been drinking white Russians all night. He's about two or so inches shorter than me and scrawny, weighing in at about 130lbs. I pushed him and started to cock my fist. He fell straight to the ground against the driver side door. "I fly out in the morning. I'll get a cab back to the house and a cab out first thing in the morning." I wanted to hit him; it would have let out a quarter century of anger towards the bastard. However, I refrained.

I got back in to town the next day, Sunday. I almost forgot about that plasma he'd bought me... "It" said, "We need to go pick it up before he cancels the order!"

I said, "Damn right! That's a fifteen-hundred-dollar TV for crying out load!" The store he bought it from was closed when my flight got in, so the very next morning, I called in to work late and waited for the store to open. It was seven-fifty-nine in the morning! "I have an order to pick up."

The sales person said, "Sure, go to pick-up area C, and it will be out in a few minutes." I picked it up, and, before I'd even had time to unpack the box it was in, my phone blew up. It was my dad...IGNORE! Let's get this bad-boy hooked up now. He left me a lengthy voice mail, explaining how he tried to cancel the order but it had already been picked up. He demanded I return it immediately.

Really, you think I was going to return my birthday present because my Dad was being an Indian giver? Nope, I wanted to see what it was like to play the Wii on fifty inches of high definition plasma. Thanks, Dad!

"Where am I?"

So I never mentioned that my mother in-law was a speech pathologist. Do you know what a pathologist really means? Here ya go: *Pathology* (pah-THOL-lo-gee) is the science dealing with the theory or causation of a disease. Please! The woman is a disease herself! How can one disease help another disease? I didn't say I was perfect, dammit! A divorce is a disease in itself. Think about it. It hits you, and the average one lasts about a year. If that's not a disease then what is it?

This woman teaches young children how to communicate with other people. She works with children with autism and other types of mental deficiencies. After hearing about the woman, would you want your kid in the same room with her? "What! Your pappa has a beer after work and your mother and father argue every once in a while? Come on, little student, let's go talk to this nice-looking officer. He can help straighten this out."

I think the only talent the woman has is her meatloaf. She makes the meanest meatloaf in the world! I've sh*t myself many a times after eating it. Maybe she was trying to get me with Cyanide, and that's what gave me the runs. I still don't know. It was good sh*t though! I mean the food! I suppose if she would have done that, she probably would have been caught somehow. How does a perfectly-healthy twenty-six-year-old suddenly die after having dinner at the in-laws? There would have been an autopsy on my body; they would have found a diarrhea-tic called "Its mother."

I did really enjoy the time with my mother in-law's mother. She was the best. That little woman weighed eighty pounds soaking wet. She never remembered where she was within five minutes, due to Alzheimer's or Dementia. That's probably why we got along. I never knew where I was going when I was married to "It" either. I just knew that I was going where "It" told me to. I went there, and then said, "Where am I?"

"It" and "Its" mother decided to do us a favor. They decided to clean out our basement. This sounds like a nice gesture, but all of my stuff was down there. "It" really never let me keep much in our livable square footage, rather, in our storage. Needless to say, I lost the two best porno's that I think I have ever bought. One I bought for the enjoyment of my wife and me, which consequently I never had the opportunity to enjoy. It was called, "The art of the blow-job." We tried to get kinky with it a few times, and so I thought I might enlighten her. I picked up this mind-rippling movie from a local porn shop. Of course, I watched it to see which part to fast forward to. I figured my wife wouldn't want to sit and watch blow-jobs for an entire hour and a half. I still have not experienced that part to this day. It would have been a great lesson for "It," though.

I sure wlsh sodomy was legal in the United States

Visits are always the best. So, I told you I bought that expensive Baby Einstein seat. Well, my little one loved it. I thought I'd be nice and cordial over the phone text messaging with "It." It just never happens that way though. I'm always nice. I have to be. The woman has me by the nuts, literally. If I say one thing she doesn't like, she would have me arrested. How does that work, anyway? This was supposed to be a free country. It's more of a socialistic type of country if you ask me.

I took a picture of our little girl playing in the new toy I bought her. I then asked "It," "Does she have one of these in Bum F*ck, Egypt?"

She replied in a very combative tone, "It better not have wheels."

For crying out loud! Wheels! I'm not taking her to the Indy 500! We're in my living room for crying out loud! "No, it does not," I said.

She then asked me if she had eaten, and I replied, "A little. She didn't want the jar food so I made her a bottle."

Hot Damn! She didn't like that at all, and she quickly sent another text message complaining about that. "You know I breast feed her, Andrew!"

Chill out, "It."

My attorney has tried telling her attorney that I do not need supervision, and we have letters from paid professionals affirming it. She still will not let me have my daughter for more than two hours at a time. It is ultimately up to her until the judge orders it. Then, if she decides to not follow it, she is in contempt of court. The woman's a schoolteacher. Do you really think she's going to break the law? The worst thing I have ever seen the woman do was make an illegal left turn on a busy street. I told her that she couldn't turn, but do you think she listened? Nope, and we got side swiped by a truck and then pulled over in to a parking lot. She was crying. I got out of the car and it did about two thousand worth of damage to hers, however, the truck was fine. It messed up one of the nerf bars, but not bad. The whole way home she cried about it and made it seem like it was my fault. I forgot to tell you, I'm telepathic and also have the ability to control someone's mind. I learned how to do this right before "It" and I got married. Why else do you think she decided to marry me? Her mom sure didn't want that. At least at the time, though, she seemed OK with me marrying her daughter. It just took a year or so for her to finally crack and go ape-sh*t about it.

We have court next week. I am one hundred percent sure "It" is not going to like the outcome. Not only is she going to have to continue to drive almost a thousand miles a week to bring our daughter to my house, but I'm hopefully going to start to get her overnights. That's gonna chap her ass like a nasty sunburn, the kind that prohibits you from sitting down comfortably. I sure wish sodomy were legal in the United States. I'd love to throw "It's" mother down and plug it right up her ass.

Til Death Do Us Part

I'm going to a wedding in a few hours. Really? A wedding! Why am I going to a wedding? I'm the last person you should see at a wedding. My thoughts about a wedding include nasty, horrible words with blood spilled on the pages.

The only reason I'm going is because a friend of mine didn't want to go by herself. I agreed, as long as I could bring my iPod. Do you seriously think I want to hear wedding vows spoken aloud again, for at least the next twenty years? No! My phone has the radio and is an iPod. I have small earpieces that are very inconspicuous. We will sit in the back and wait for the reception. Those are fun, however. Usually, the bridesmaids are hot, at least until you get through the two inches of mascara and eye shadow. It'll be my luck, though, that they're all overweight and ugly. I have nothing against overweight women. I've had my fair share back in the day. But when ugly and overweight come together, they usually don't make a nice pair. There's really nothing a woman can do to fix it, either. Maybe I'm just a chauvinistic pig. But I like it and it works, at least for now...

I wish I could tell you I come up with this , but I don't. But it really does happen to me!

It was nine thirty in the morning...The wedding was enough to make me puke. The pastor wouldn't shut up during the service. "To have and to hold, for better, for worse, till death do you part." Really? Who came up with that? I showed you the statistics. How many people take this seriously anymore? These aren't vows to most people. They're just words.

I'm not the one who wants this divorce. The only reason that I'm the plaintiff is because I knew she would file first in Bum F*ck, Egypt. Think about it. I would have lost every single battle I had won. I would not get to see my daughter at all if it was in Bum F*ck, Egypt. I love "It." But I had to choose. Do I play stupid and ignorant, or do I play realistic and rational? "It" has tried everything in the book to extinguish me from our daughter's life. I hope one day "It" looks in the mirror and feels some remorse for what she did. However, I have prevailed. I want to reconcile with "It" because that's what's right. But it takes two to tango. That just goes to show you, people are not always who they say they are. My wife told me a thousand times that divorce was never an option. To me, it's not an option either. An option means more than one choice. I have no other choices at this time. I could drop the case completely, but I'd be a moron if I did. She'd pick it right back up, except a hundred and fifty miles away in Bum F*ck, Egypt. Then I'd be right back to square one. I took a vow and, well, at least for me, I meant every word. "It" must not have, because the words "Till death do you part" have no meaning to the woman whatsoever. I so badly wanted to peep up and say, "Till death us do part, or if she gets mad and your mother says it's OK... then we can get divorced."

The reception was just as bad as the wedding. It was only three years ago when we were the ones in the middle of that wedding party table. Looking at the wedding party made me drink my captain and coke just that much quicker, in hopes of distorting the images that were coming to mind. I looked over at the gal I had come with and told her we needed to leave. We did. We left before they even served food. I can't believe I was dragged to a wedding. It took about everything I had in there not to cry. Oh wait! I was told that I am emotionless. Maybe those weren't tears, but rather a short-lived anaphylactic reaction to the warm, pungent air in the church.

I have won in excess of $100,000,000 in the last month

I told you that this entire thing has cost me about $40,000. Let's do some quick math here and see where it all went. My attorney has cost me about $10,000. I had a $2,000 psychological evaluation. My parent coaches and many different supervisors have cost me about $2,500. I had a substance and abuse evaluation, which ran $500. "It" extorted $9,500...Where are we at, here?

$10,000+$2,000+$2,500+$500+$9,500: OK so we're at $24,500 hard cost. Now we need to bring in the aspect that "It" stole my entire life and did so legally. I had to buy another vehicle and that ran about $5,000. My short lease on the apartment was about $3,500. I had to buy new furniture that ran about $3,000 with my daughter's complete bedroom set included. I've paid about $2,000 in child support thus far. That's around $38,000, and I know I forgot to include something else. It'll hit me when this chapter is up! So we are definitely over $40,000. How many people do you know that can take a hit like that and then write a book about it?

I got an email, and I think all of my problems are solved at least financially! Please excuse the grammar, as it is not mine. I copied and pasted it from my Yahoo account. See below.

THE PRESIDENCY OFFICE

Aso Rock villa, Asokoro District, Abuja

Direct Confidential telephone number +234 80 377 807 94

Email: (lt_fdukur@mail.mn)

Nigeria Foreign payment allocation Transaction/ delivery codes (/PRFGN/ FEC/ESSX) strictly follow these security instructions; disregard any replica of this letter without the actual security code. Clinical diplomatic package immunity risk free delivery payment Fund Beneficiary, you have to observe the following nstructions.

I am Lt. General Fidelis Dukur, special adviser to President Goodluck Ebele Jonathan on foreign matters, I am delighted to inform you that the contract panel that just concluded it seating in Abuja, released your name among contractors/inheritors of Nigeria national petroleum corporation over-invoiced lottery raffle draw to benefit from the Diplomatic risk free Immunity Payment. This Panel was primarily delegated to investigate Manipulated contracts lottery and inheritance claims, contracts and over-invoiced payment as the negative effects has eaten deep into The Economy of our dear country. Disregard any replica of this message without the presidential allocation code as stated above. However, we wish to bring to your notice that your contract/ inheritance lottery profile is still reflecting in our central Computeronic presidential system as an unpaid contract/inheritance during auditing excise.

Your payment file was forwarded To my office by the auditors as unclaimed fund, we wish to use this mediumto inform you that for the time being, Federal Government of Nigeria have stopped further payment through bank to bank transfer, payment by draft or ATM except on some special instructions, due to foreign beneficiary numerous petitions to United Nations, FBI, CIA and international police against Nigeria on wrong payment and diversion of foreign funds to different accounts.

In this regards, we are going to release your foreign part payment of 6.7 Million USD through an accredited security clinical shipping company, I will secure every needed documents to cover the money from all illegal odds. Note: The funds are coming on 2 security-proof boxes, wrap with a security foil. The boxes are sealed with synthetic nylon seal and padded with machine. Please you don't have to worry for anything, as the transaction is 100% risk free. The boxes are coming with Diplomatic agent who will accompany the boxes to your house address. All you need to do now is to send to me your full house address and your identity such as, international Passport or drivers license and your mobile phone and telephone number, The Diplomatic Attach will travel with it. He will call you immediately he arrives your country's airport. I hope you understand me. You have not been able to receive these funds simply because those crooks you are dealing refused to tell you the truth about the origin of the funds rather the present a case which established wrong and deceptive payment approach in other to riff you off. Your email address happens to be among the lucky winners of this lottery contract/inheritance claim. Those people sent you manipulated forged documents that are not for the release of these particular funds and most times the increase the sum just to attract you.

Note: The diplomat does not know the original contents of the boxes. What I declared to them as the contents is Photographic Film Materials for security reasons. I did not declare money to them please. If they call you and ask you the contents please tell them the same thing Ok. Call me on my direct +234 80 377 807 94) Email : (lt_fdukur@mail.mn). Forget your past now that I have contacted you.

I will let you know how far I have gone with the arrangement. I will secure all the approved clearances for smooth delivery which will make it scale through every security and customs checking points all over the world without hitch. Confirm the receipt of this message and Send the requirements to me immediately you receive this message. Please I need urgent reply because the boxes are schedule to live as soon as we hear from you. Call me immediately. I am with the foreign payment diplomatic delivery diskette, you will not receive one dollar cent outside me, is impossible, I will advise you to forget whatever dealings you have at the moment and concentrate on my proposals now that I have contacted you. The new president has good intentions so don?t bother or worry yourself since all legitimacy will be Observed. Call me or get back to me through this email address. Is imperative to inform you that some crooks have started impersonating on the name of the new Nigeria president to advance there extortion, please disregard any message impersonating office of the presidency, central bank, others, and others since government has handed over the foreign payment redialed disk to me. I know you may or not have gone through past experience but beware of any proposal in and outside Nigeria. Just give this opportunity a trial and you will not regret knowing me rather you will show gratitude for my kind gesture. Call me for further enquiry but keep this letter as secret.

1) Your Full Name
2) Phone and Fax Numbers
3) Address Where You Will Like to Receive Your Funds
4) Your Age and Current Occupation
5) A Copy of Your Personal Identification

Congratulations.
Best Regards,
Lt General Fidelis Dukur (Rtd),

How do these foreign spammers get away with this? I get at least one of these a week. Do people seriously give them their information? It's probably safe, though. I wouldn't honestly think that there's anyone out there that would use your information in a felonious manner.

Did you read that? Come on, man, at least learn how to speak my language, if you don't want it to go straight to my spam folder. I have tried turning them in to the dot gov web site. Do you think I get a response? Please! They don't care one iota about it. I'm sure there are people out there dumb enough to actually reply. That's where Uncle Sam needs to step in and take care of his parental duties as the governor of our so-called free world.

I have won in excess of $100,000,000 in the last month from various places that I have been contacted by. Maybe it's time to follow up on them and get reimbursed for this divorce. I have also spent trillions of dollars renovating this house I bought to flip. The basement is damn near complete. I saw this wire hanging from the corner of the ceiling basement. What was it? I figured it must go to the telephone jack that I tore out upstairs. I went upstairs and grabbed a pair of heavy-duty snips and proceeded back to the basement. The wire looked trashy as all get out, just dangling from a brand new ceiling with recessed lighting that cost me a fortune. I pulled it through the drywall about as far as it would let me go. I then cut both ends with the snips. I left the wire on the ground right by the stairs on the brand new carpet I just had installed.

It was the beginning of Fall. I kept my air conditioning to a frugal seventy-five degrees. Was it hot in here or was I starting my menstrual cycle? I walked over to the thermometer and flicked on the air conditioning, grabbed a soda, and sat down to watch some television. The air conditioning didn't kick on once. I sighed. "I'll call someone out in the morning to have a look at it." The next day, I got on Craig's List and found a free estimate, after calling some larger companies and having them tell me that their diagnosis would cost me a hundred bucks. Free estimates are always the way to go; the only problem with free estimates is that you never know who is coming into your house. For all you know, you could have invited a 300 lb. transvestite serial killer over. The guy was actually very professional and did his tests. He couldn't figure it out. He said, "Everything seems to be operating well; it must be your control box." He went upstairs and we put new batteries in it, but that didn't work, either. I tell ya, if it's not one thing, it's another! Back to the basement we went, and he said, "BINGO!" He pointed to the wire on the carpet. "Someone cut your electrical wire running to the thermometer upstairs! Who would have done that?"

Do you really think I was going to fess up to that? I'm a man, and no one witnessed it but Doug! That's probably why he wouldn't stop meowing. He was probably trying to save me a headache. "I did just have carpet thrown in the other day! I'll bet you that those asses thought they'd be funny and cut my electrical cord for the thermometer! How much will ya charge me to fix it, Sir?" I should listen to Doug more!

"It was two minutes into it; she looked up..."are you close?"

Marriage isn't that bad of a gig. It's quite comforting knowing that the love of your life is coming home soon or you are coming home to her. I'm not as mean as this book portrays me. I am a lonely guy. I will probably always be that way, too. I have no intentions of ever getting married, ever again. You're probably thinking, "Yeah, right." But honestly, I am different than most. "It" has taken every bit of love out of me. All except that for my precious garbling baby. That love is the only thing that has given me the energy to get up in the morning. Life is a struggle, but all you need is the love of a little one to keep your wits about you. People that are childless do not understand that love.

Today is Sunday, and it appears I am not going to get my precious garbling baby today. I sent "It" a message explaining that my supervisor had to run an errand during the visit that would take approximately thirty minutes. "It" said this was not acceptable. She replied, "The order states that you need a supervisor, and I want to follow it." I have multiple letters from paid child supervisors and counselors detailing my desire to be a father, furthermore bluntly saying that I am very fit based on hours upon hours of supervision over the last few months.

This was not good enough for "It." "It" has been using our daughter as leverage against me to play the court system. Most women get away with it, I hear. Not her. I will not allow her to use our daughter in such a negative way. Have you ever heard anyone say, "A child doesn't need their father?" I didn't think so. She must have read it on another website verified by Norton Anti-virus. Just because it's verified by a virus software doesn't make it the truth. I will give her this, though, the first one she found on fertility hit the hammer right on the nail. Don't get me wrong, we had a lot of good times in that marriage. I remember our first anniversary like it was an hour ago. I couldn't figure out what to do, so I asked a few buddies. One of them recommended that we go to a bed and breakfast. This buddy that recommended it happened to be the buddy of mine that "It" despised. Come on now; every wife hates one of her husband's friends. She still doesn't know he gave me the idea.

I refer to "Its" hometown as Bum F*ck, Egypt, but that's not the only one out there, though. I really don't mind going to an occasional BFE small town in the middle of nowhere. This Bum F*ck, Egypt, however, was actually enjoyable. We got in the car. We took my shiny Chrysler 300M. It was a nice ride! It had a wood grain dash, black leather interior, tinted windows, you name it. It could do anything but pour you a cup of coffee. The place was about an hour or so in to Iowa. A tiny little town called Pocahontas.

The town really wasn't much of a town. The gas cost almost a dollar more there than back home, I think, because the gas companies hated driving out there. The one tiny grocery store was about as limited on groceries as the tiny gas station down the street from my house. A Quick Trip or

Bucky's would have been nice. At least you have all the food groups to choose from for the most part.

It took us another hour to find the bed and breakfast. It was actually nice. It was located on about three hundred acres; part of it was a farm. It would have been the perfect spot for those guys I had working for me to grow pot. We checked in and got the food schedule. They had little, tiny condo-looking buildings that were the rooms for the guests. For once in our marriage, I think I finally did something right. She loved it. My cell phone didn't work out there; maybe that's why she liked it. Either way I liked it too.

We actually planned on going back the next year, but 2008 was a bad year. I lost my grandmother. She was the one who raised me. Shortly after her death I got the DUI. I was in jail/work release over the three months of our anniversary in 2009 for the DUI. So 2009 wasn't going to work either. I really wish we had gone back, though. That place was as calm and serene as they come. We had a few other nice excursions. We went to Corpus Christi for our honeymoon. That cost a pretty penny. We had been gifted a lot of money from the wedding, so that helped out. There was this little place called Docs down there. It had to have been the neatest restaurant I have ever been to, even to this day. It was right on the ocean. It started on the shore and stretched out hundreds of feet over the gulf. We shared a fishbowl, and I managed to talk the waitress into letting me steal it as a memoir of our intimacy.

"Its" idea of a fun excursion included sleeping on a blowup mattress in her parents' basement. Their bedroom was above us. I felt like I was in high school all over again. I tried to get it on with her down there late at night, a few times, but she wouldn't have it. Come on, woman!

We're newlyweds; live a little. They're sleeping and her dad's a bigger guy; you could have heard him coming from a mile away. My mother in-law would have had a stroke, but I doubt she would have come down, either. I will say this with a large smile on my face, though. I did talk "It" into a quick blow-job down in their basement. "It" was two minutes into it; she looked up…"are you close?"

Father's rights in all seriousness... you might just become "It."

All states are exactly the same, basically, when it comes to a mother and father's parenting rights. This judge I happen to have, which is deciding the future relationship my daughter will have with her father is typical in these types of proceedings. I have done absolutely nothing to prove myself unfit as a father. The last time I checked, it takes two people to make a baby. So, therefore, it should take two to raise a baby, and those two should be the same two that conceived her. Courts, however, do not see it that way. They view fathers as a negation to every statement in terms of parenting. Let's face it; divorce causes bitter animosity towards both parties. Even though I would jump at the opportunity to remain committed to my vows, I still am very angry about the situation. I have values and morals when it comes to the vows I took on that day not that long ago. But when two people's values are different minded, when it comes to taking a vow, that tends to birth a divorce, as well.

My attorney told me about a friend that invited him to their wedding. He declined their invitation because he knew that they would be in contact with him regarding representation in divorce court. He went on to tell me that he didn't want to visually see two people take vows that he knew would be broken. Then he said that it would be within a year or two and, of course, they would have their own precious garbling baby. How sad. The magnitude of divorce with children is unimaginable. It is not physically, emotionally, or even psychologically possible for someone to understand this without having experienced it. The concept of it makes a person empathetic, but that's about it.

In this story, Andrew Zeebs did absolutely nothing to warrant the behavior of "It." If "It" did not wish to continue their marriage vows then she should have done so in a mature way. I'm not quite sure there's a mature way to divorce someone, but it could have been done differently. As for myself, I truly hate having to make "It" drive so many miles a week to deliver *our* precious garbling baby to her father. But what must be done, must be done. I have absolutely no idea how much "Its" mother has spent on the entire proceedings to this date. But I can tell you, it has to be somewhat close to mine, at least the attorney-fee portion. "It" did not have to re-buy "Its" life as I did. Rather, "Its" mother did so-lovingly take such an expense as her own.

In one affidavit, "Its" mother stated that she was not trying to plot against me and remove me from my daughter's life. But this situation has affirmed my long-time belief that actions speak louder than words. I am more angry at "Its" mother than any other person in the entire world.

How would you feel about your mother in-law taking your entire family away from you without regret? You were born with the same components of a heart that I was, so I'm sure it would piss you off. Here's some advice, don't be. Because "It" was the one who let that happen. We live in a free world, which is hypocritical of our country in many ways. Impulsiveness brings a horrid future. Remorse and regret are so kindly bestowed upon you later down the line, whether a year or a lifetime. They will knock on your door. Usually when they knock, it's one of those knocks that you have mixed emotions about answering. You have to answer the door, though, because they will not stop knocking. At that point, you are in my shoes.

My biggest mistake, honestly, was moving out of the house in hopes of remedying the situation through separation. Have you ever heard of anything fixing itself? That's exactly what separation implies. Two people take a time-out to fix the situation. That's when things always get worse. You may have heard of people that have done it successfully, but they are few and far between. Separation brings a freedom to problems and masks their presence through absence.

Everyone I talk to says that this is just a "blip in the road." That's one blip I wouldn't wish upon anyone. It's hard to imagine that the divorce rate has increased one percent, per year, for the last twenty-plus years. Does this tell you where our country is heading? Seriously? In twenty years, we're all looking at it. You'll be a minority to have not experienced it. For now, though, live "It," love "It," learn "It," and lastly enjoy "It." Whether your "It" is a man or a woman, or you are a man or a woman, I recommend sitting down with your partner and having the "It" discussion. Because if you don't, you might just become "It."

The judge ordered the removal of my penis?

My alarm went off at promptly eight o'clock in the morning. I crawled out of bed. If you're wondering, I'm still sleeping on that futon. I haven't made myself go buy a real bed. I have the money, believe it or not, but I just hate shopping. I'm a cheap ass, as well. I'd probably start looking in department stores and settle on something off Craig's List. If it weren't for Craig's List, guys like me would be lost. I wouldn't have the slightest clue where you can go buy a bed, without paying out an exorbitant amount for it.

I had to pick up a letter from my attorney's office and get it signed by one of the supervisors I've had in the past.

"It" wrote an affidavit for the courts, praying the supervision continued. "It" is trying everything in "Its" power to make my life as difficult as possible. In one part of the affidavit, she said this about one of my supervisors. "The supervisor brought our daughter to me late, and said that she had just got out of the shower." Really "It." She brought her out two minutes late, a whole one hundred and twenty seconds! She then continued. "If Andrew and her are on that friendly of terms, I doubt her creditability to judge whether or not the visits should be unsupervised." Really, "It." You forgot to mention that the supervisor told you she was in the shower because I told her she could use it. Doug pissed on her. For real! I didn't do her. I'm not lying here, either. I told her she could use my shower. She was holding little Doug and Doug decided that would be the place to let 'em loose. It was kind of surprising, but not really. The little guy doesn't always use his litter box. I've come home to cat crap stuck in my brand new carpet. I have a short creme shag carpet. The only thing I can do is cut it out with a pair of scissors. He either does it in the middle of the night or when I'm not looking, because I have never caught him.

She signed an affidavit denying the allegations and also made some recommendations about the visits, which were in my favor. To tell you the truth, now that "It" said that about her, I kinda wish I had done her. She's got fake tits; you can totally tell. How many women do you know that have perfectly round breasts and nipples right in the middle of them? OK, I did see her nipples protruding from her shirt. What kinda guy doesn't check that out, though? I'd ask her, but that might be an awkward conversation. I will tell you, though, she is a very good person and she has helped me out a ton during this entire ordeal.

I also had two other affidavits from other people telling the judge that I am a very good dad. They were the two other supervisors I had to have. Then "It" says that the only reason they said I was a good dad was because I paid them. The judge ordered a parent coach and a licensed mental health practitioner. Do you think they work for free? Dear lord baby Jesus, now what?

Two o'clock rolled around. I threw on some dress clothes and headed out the door. Like I told you, I usually park the Beamer in the parking garage downtown. I don't need another parking ticket because the hearing lasted longer than I anticipated. I walked into the courtroom and took a seat. "It" was nowhere to be seen. That's interesting. This was a big one; the hearing was very important. The judge sentenced a guy who got a DUI to probation. I wish I'd had this judge when I got mine. I probably wouldn't have my precious garbling baby now, though. I don't regret having her one bit, but "It" was the one who talked me into it a lot sooner than I planned on having her.

I stepped out of the courtroom and, sure enough, there "It" was, tightly concealed behind a small wall, sitting on a bench in the middle of the district-court hallway. I looked at "It" from a distance, and she appeared to be wearing a gift from my late grandmother, a pink cardigan. I couldn't believe that she had the audacity to wear that to one of these hearings! How do you think the woman who gave her that would feel about her stealing my daughter from me and doing all of the stuff she has done? Plus, this was the same woman who raised me. It does sadden me, though; she never had the opportunity to hold my precious garbling baby. Grandma would have loved her so much. Consequently, I did happen to talk "It" into naming her middle name after her. Our daughter never met her grandmother on my side; with whom she now shares the same name, but she will hear stories.

My attorney finally walked in about three minutes before the hearing. I could tell this was going to be a long one, too. He had me sign a few documents and told me to go take a seat in the courtroom. By then, "It" was in "Its" usual spot, about two seats down in the back row. The courtroom was empty. It was just the two of us in there. Now I didn't tell you this, but I have A.D.D. I have been told so, at least by "It". I couldn't keep still. It was just "It" and me in a thousand-square-foot courtroom. The only sound was that of a fan, which was very consistent, yet very soft. I sat directly two rows up from her once again. Except this time, I didn't feel like being the annoying type and sitting right in front of "It". So I sat an extra row forward.

Occasionally, I would glance towards her, and she would look the other way. She sat as if she didn't even recognize me. I just can't do that. If I know someone, they always know that I know them in one way or another. "It" was colder than a bag of peas that had been left in the deep freeze for two weeks. Expressionless, motionless, and also emotionless "It" sat. This was getting way too intense for me. I stepped out into the hallway and paced the corridors for a solid twenty minutes. I tried striking up a conversation with a guard at the other end of the hall, but I could tell he didn't want to talk to me. I then continued to pace the hallway. I counted the tiles and stepped off the footage. Impressive. The hallway on the fourth floor was a whopping 883 square feet, and that was only a quarter of it. The courthouse was older than dirt and had antique crown molding. I toured it when I was a kid. The thing is bigger than the biggest mall in town. I felt like an ant knowing a shoe the size of the moon was about to come down on me. Almost two hours later, after going back in to the courtroom and feeling the intensity of quietness, I had to step out multiple times. Her attorney stepped out and motioned her to the hallway. Where was mine? I overheard a tiny bit of the conversation between "It" and "Its" attorney. I still couldn't tell you what had transpired, though.

Finally, mine steps out, and he could see the anticipation on my face. "We did good for the most part." Who likes hearing that? "For the most part." What...so I just lost my dick too? "It" had both of my testicles legally removed, and now the judge ordered the removal of my penis?

The judge actually removed supervision, and "Its" attorney gave every plea in the book not to. I bet she offered to blow him in the chambers, too. He wouldn't have it, it seemed. She's really not a very good looking woman, either. I feel bad for her husband, if she's got one. How can a woman divorce attorney even have a husband? I know I'd be scared to marry a woman divorce attorney. If you think I'm getting done dirty here, imagine what she'd do to her husband if she went through a divorce?

I now get my daughter a few more hours a week, and the supervision is removed. I told you that "It" would be livid. I sure wish I could have stayed in that hallway for that conversation. The final date to finish the case is soon. For now, I have to accept that overnights are not quite here yet. But if I keep pressing, I will get them after that date. I still have to drive to Bum F*ck, Egypt, yup! Lovely Bum F*ck, Egypt, and I only get to see her for an hour there. My weekend visits are longer, though, and it's still every weekend. "It" still has to drive as well. Do you really think the so-honorable judge lowered my child support either? It's still the same per month. He doesn't care that I'm a full-time student. I wasn't asking for it to be removed, just lowered a little. That was based on $40,000 per year.

That's OK, though. I will get to play with my precious garbling baby unsupervised a few more hours a week. I have learned not to be angry about it. It is what it is and, as long as I am diligently trying to be a part of my precious garbling baby's life, then I am doing the most I can do with what hand has been dealt to me. As a father and soon to be ex-husband at the choice of "It," I will never give up. Ever.

Don't you love our judicial system?

The unsupervised visits are great. I finally get to enjoy fatherhood in privacy. I received a phone call at eight o'clock in the morning. My realtor said, "We have a showing in one hour!" Ho -Ho- Hold up, here! "A showing? I can't I have my daughter today. He said, "We need to show it, Andrew; otherwise, it won't sell."

"OK, I'll make it work. What time do I need to leave and when can I come back?" He told me to leave and that I could return home at ten o'clock. I text messaged "It" to bring my daughter a little later. You think I get a reply? Nope.

I got in the car and went up the street to some little diner and got breakfast. I was half asleep, because the night before I had gone to a concert. My head was pounding. "Can I get that country fried steak and eggs?" Damn, that was a good breakfast! I had three cups of coffee and ate. I knew that, even though "It" hadn't responded to my message, "It" would be there when I asked. I turned the corner and saw her car down the street. I floored it. She was parked on my side of the street, right next to my driveway. "It" was sitting in "Its" car, by "Itself." I slowed down to a stop, my driver-side window next to "Its." I shook my head then lip synched, "I love you." I think she was kind of stunned.

I couldn't see much of her, even though we were only a couple feet away. I then put it in reverse and backed up in to the driveway. I had to have someone exchange our daughter because "It" is still hung up on that bogus protection order. I think the real reason that "It" didn't want to come anywhere close to me is because of all of the crap "It" has put me through. Like I told you before, would you want to look someone in the eyes while holding his testicles in one hand and a severely-dull, bloody knife in the other?

My exchange person showed up and brought my precious garbling baby to Daddy. She crawled about three feet during the visit. I think I might have heard "Da?" Of course, only from the corner of my ear and so fast that I can't confirm it. She garbles a lot, so it may have been that too.

The end of the visit always comes too soon. My exchange person came back a few minutes before my precious garbling baby's departure. I packed her things and changed her diaper. I'd hate for "It" to go to the courts and tell them I sent her back with a wet one. I received a text message about five minutes after she left, asking about naps and feedings. Then I got one that said, "Did she bump her head?" She tried telling me there was a red spot on the side of her face. Really! It never ends! Luckily, I had eyewitnesses, so if "It" tries to go to court with another lie, I can prove "It" wrong once more.

Have you ever met a person with such an intensity to ruin a father-daughter bond? I flicked the television on that evening. HBO apparently got in touch with "It." There was a documentary on about a pregnant woman who was beaten by her husband. They just forgot the part where the police were called and let the wife beater go as the wife lied in tears without one bruise. This is comical, though, about a week or so after-wards mine did that; she went to court and told the judge she had bruises. The judge asked for evidence. "It" didn't have anything to bring to the table. Don't you love our judicial system?

(fubar'd)

I'll have to tell you, it's been a tough week. You gotta hear this! So "It" cancels a couple of visits, lies about my precious garbling baby being sick, and then tries to get me arrested. Did I just say arrested? I think so. "It" claimed that I got home at the same time the first unsupervised visit was to commence (which I did); however, "It" went on to say that I pulled my BMW bumper to bumper to with "Its" bumper, then rolled down the window, threw something at "Its" car, screamed profanities, and made faces. The irony in this, is that "It" still decided to let me have the visit and then, six hours later, "It" called the police and told them that I had violated the protection order. The police asked "It" why "It" was at my house. "It" went on to say that "It" was instructed by "Its" attorney to come to my house. When asked for evidence, "It" didn't have anything to produce in "Its" offense.

What is wrong with that woman? This woman has tried to get me arrested at least twice that I know of. This time it took me two days to find out that she tried to get me arrested. We're talking about the same woman who brought me dinner and pussy every evening I spent at my office on work release. How twisted is that? She stood by me when I goofed up and got the DUI then was sentenced to work-release in jail. No...she's or "It's" trying to put me back in the same place. Just when you think it can't get any more f*cked up beyond all recognition (fubar'd), "It" shows you that you're wrong.

I found out that "It" was lying about my precious garbling baby being sick. I finally coaxed "It" into giving me the phone number to the doctor she took her to. I called and signed a HIPAA form and received my baby's patient records. The oh-so-kind nurse was ever so nice to even scratch a note from the doctor on it. The note read, "Mr. Zeebs called our office regarding his daughter's visit to our office. He stated that he had regular visitation on the weekends, and I informed him after speaking to the doctor that there was no reason why she could not travel."

How nice is that. I might have to give her a hug when I find myself in Bum F*ck, Egypt, again.

"It" and "Its" mother must have sat down and had a heart to heart. If that's what you call premeditating a sadistic plan in Bum F*ck, Egypt. I sure wish I had been there for that one. That would have been another interesting conference of "It" and "Its" mother's minds. "It" is losing "Its" ass off in court, and "It" knows it. Truthfully speaking, nobody wins in a divorce, especially with children involved. You're sure to lose something. My attorney called it something like an expensive win, where the costs outweigh the prize won. You see, I'm on my way to getting regular visitation as a normal man with a penis is usually awarded. However, it's just taking a long time to get it.

I got kind of frustrated in learning about the incident I was almost arrested for. I sent "Its" mother a great chapter in this book. I sent her a picture of the cover and one of the last chapters of the book. I'm sure she's gonna love it. She has no idea I wrote a book specifically devoted to the unconditionally-cold, devious feeling of animosity I have towards my beloved Mother In-Law.

I know what you're thinking; that was extreme...maybe so...but I really don't care at this point in time. If sodomy was legal...I already told you, I'd plug it right up her ass. I am, however, a law-abiding citizen. There's no harm in writing congress to get the laws of sodomy changed...is there?

Years of Age × 12 months in a year × 10 seconds = Your attention span in minutes
60 seconds in a minute

I'm sure you remember Ms. Camel Toe. Sure enough! I happened to see it again at the next parenting class. Does she not know her pussy is inhaling her oh-so-tight dress slacks like a fat kid takes down a junior whopper? I'd at least think she'd feel it. There has to be a more appropriate word for it other than camel toe, I just haven't taken an English class in a long time.

That class was an interesting one as well. I was over at my attorney's office the hour before I was to be in the class.

I jumped in the Beamer and sped to the institution where the class was held. I got out and ran in with a bag of Arby's and a Cherry Coke. I hadn't eaten all day. I was almost ready to pass out due to hunger. I walked in the double doors and went up to the floor, where the class was in session. I then found out that I was an hour late to the two-hour class. They had apparently met early and I didn't catch the memo.

There were trinkets, tape, empty prescription bottles, colored construction paper, and empty macaroni and cheese boxes on a table to the back. Ms. Camel Toe came up to me and told me to fill out a few documents and then told me to make a toy to stimulate my little one with. Really! A toy? What do you make out of empty macaroni and cheese boxes and prescription bottles? I told you I hate the store, but I think this warranted a trip to Wal-Mart. Needless to say, Wal-Mart was not an option. I forgot to mention, there were also plastic forks and knives on the back table. Who in his or her right mind gives a seven-month-old a fork and a knife to play with? It doesn't matter whether they are plastic or not, you should see how fiercely my precious garbling baby inserts her toys into her mouth.

I managed to put this together. I couldn't quite tell you what it was, though. All I know is that there were no sharp ends on it, and it rattles when you shake it.

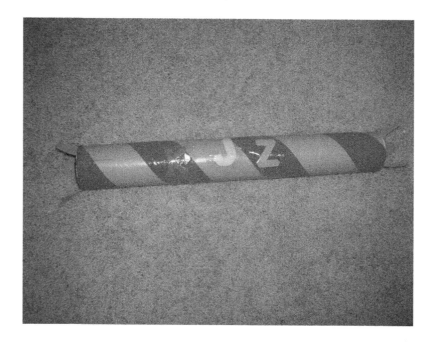

That's also the beautiful short creme shag carpet that Doug loves to take a dump on. But seriously, what is that in the picture? I made the damn thing, but I have no idea what you could do with it. They say a baby's attention span is about ten seconds for every month of its life. I really don't think I could keep her entertained for a whole seventy seconds with that thing. After about ten seconds or so, she'd look up at me and think, what are you doing, Dad? I'm sure the verbiage would be different, but you get my point.

I did think that was interesting, though. Babies' attention spans are ten seconds for every month of their age. I think that applies to some adults too. I can't speak for you, but I know that I can't sit and listen to a rattle toy for an hour. Let's do some math, here's the equation:

$$\frac{\text{Years of Age} \times 12 \text{ months in a year} \times 10 \text{ seconds}}{60 \text{ seconds in a minute}} = \text{Your attention span in minute}$$

With this equation, my attention spans comes up to fifty-two minutes. That sounds about right. My college classes are about fifty minutes apiece. They must have known this equation when my academic adviser figured out my class schedule. How else do I have a 3.0 GPA?

That doesn't mean I still don't hate my mother in-law...

I believe that both parents should equally share custody, unless one proves to be unfit. I have proven the exact opposite and have had more than plenty of opportunity to back out of this. But, as I told you before, any man that does needs to take a look in the mirror and ask himself why? I am fortunate enough to have the means to pursue it as quickly as I am. However, in light of all truth, most men out there are not. That does not mean you have to throw in the towel. What that means is that time is money. Patience is a virtue that you need to have, whether or not you are a man or a woman experiencing this or having experienced it.

As a lot of you know, it is a very painful process. Divorce and custody proceedings have the tendency to make or break a person. There are laws out there to protect a person's rights. It takes a lot of creativity and love to make them work in your favor. With love, patience, diligence, and perseverance, you will survive. In my case, I was thrown to the dogs. I have taken each and every single last one of them and eaten them for my precious garbling baby.

I'm not special. I was not born with an additional feature that everyone else wasn't. I just took a hard look in the mirror and asked myself what was important in life. What makes the world turn ever so gently enough to give us a beautiful day, yet such a dark night? I still don't know the answers. I will never know all the answers, at least as long as my twisted, broken ass is still here.

One thing I do know, what you bring into this world is ultimately your responsibility, until you leave it. I truly hope this was somewhat of an inspiring account of a father's drive to ensure his role in his daughter's life. I added a few things that I have experienced to give you the full picture. Believe it or not, you are affected by everything around you, even that gas station attendant whom you saw for only a brief ninety seconds; while you were in such a hurry to get in, gas up, and get out. People are too busy with their lives to take even a second and step out of it to see what is going on around them.

I am sure I will be victorious in my pursuit to father my precious garbling baby. I am not fighting my wife, rather my mother-in-law. A lot of people have a hard time understanding that. But when someone is manipulated to the point that "It" has been, they tend not to make their own decisions; rather, they let the manipulator do so. The sad part about it is that even when it's staring them right in the face, they still don't see it that way.

As a husband, as I still presently am today (at least for another few weeks or so), I love my wife unconditionally and am truly regretful for having to do this to her. But my precious garbling baby deserves a father. That is what she will receive, and only time will heal my broken, twisted ass.

That doesn't mean I still don't hate my mother in-law...

And for your information, I wrote this book because I felt compelled to make my position clear to all of the people out there that have gone through this, and I hope you can relate to me. And for the rest of you, I wouldn't recommend it. It's just no fun. I'm sure we'll have more to talk about in the near future. For now, take care of "It," because you never know what "Its" mother will do...

Did you wake up and breastfeed tonight?

"Holy Crap! What in tarnation was that?" I looked over at the alarm and it displayed 1:11 AM on the dial. My wife rolled over and said in a soft tone, "Honey, what's wrong?"

I replied, "Oh nothing, just a bad dream! Babe, did you wake up and breastfeed tonight?"

Made in the USA
Middletown, DE
19 August 2020